THE SHEPHERD OF SALISBURY PLAIN

THE SHEPHERD AND MR. JOHNSON ON SALISBURY PLAIN.

THE
SHEPHERD
OF
SALISBURY PLAIN

BY

HANNAH MORE

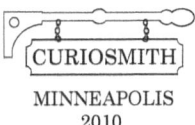

CURIOSMITH

MINNEAPOLIS
2010

PUBLISHER'S NOTE

The narrative of "Shepherd of Salisbury Plain" involved many contributors. The shepherd's name was David Saunders (1717–1796). The person called Mr. Johnson was the distinguished Dr. Stonhouse (1716–1795), also called Sir James. An often unmentioned contributor was the Rev. Henry Gauntlett (1762–1834), who grew up in the Lavington area. In 1795, Hannah More (1745–1833) composed what became the most famous of the Cheap Repository Tracts, and it was distributed in the millions.

Published by Curiosmith.
P. O. Box 390293, Minneapolis, Minnesota, 55439.
Internet: curiosmith.com.
E-mail: shopkeeper@curiosmith.com.

Previously printed by Samuel Hazard & John Marshall in 1795.

Scripture quotations are from the *Holy Bible*, King James Version.

All boldfaced footnotes were found in previous editions.
All other footnotes are added by the publisher.

Compilation, supplementary content and cover design:
Copyright © 2010 Charles J. Doe.

ISBN 978-0-9817505-5-2

Library of Congress Control Number: 2009943382

CONTENTS

HANNAH MORE.

Portrait from:
The Works of Hannah More (New York: Harper and Brothers, 1855).

HANNAH MORE

BY

HENRY JOHNSON

CHAPTER I

EARLY YEARS

AMONGST the staunchest supporters of Presbyterianism in the days of Charles II, were the Mores of Harleston, Norfolk. Glorying in the risk incurred of proscription and imprisonment, they turned their dwelling into a conventicle. Here the faithful gathered stealthily at midnight to hear the Gospel preached, whilst one of the house, with drawn sword, stood at the threshold prepared to defend with his life both minister and congregation. From this sturdy stock sprang Jacob, the father of Hannah More. He married a sensible, high-principled farmer's daughter. A family of five girls was born to them, the fourth being Hannah, whose birth occurred on the 2nd of February, 1745.

Hannah displayed remarkable precocity. Before she was four she could repeat the Catechism, much to the astonishment of the parish minister; whilst startling questions about matters far beyond her age were put to those around her. At eight her thirst for knowledge increased. Sitting on her father's knee she listened eagerly to his recital of the brave deeds of Greeks and Romans and the wise sayings of Plutarch. Sometimes her father repeated orations of classic heroes, first in the original tongue, and then in English. The interest thus excited led the child to crave for a knowledge of Latin. Her father, although averse to girls exceeding the limits of the three "R's" and a few accomplishments, yielded at length to his promising daughter's desire. This early introduction to the classics paved the way to a diligent study of Latin in later years and of the best Latin models, which greatly helped in the formation of her literary style. She also gained a little knowledge of mathematics; but Euclid had to retire in favor of the less intricate study of French. The proficiency which she afterwards acquired in this language she owed to the assiduous tuition of her eldest sister, Mary.

Before the age of twelve she began to scribble short essays and poems. Her systematic education commenced on her becoming a pupil of her sisters' boarding-school at Bristol. Here she made rapid progress, often giving convincing proof of intellectual gifts, and before long becoming qualified to assist in tuition.

In her sixteenth year she was one of Sheridan's most delighted auditors during his delivery of a course of lectures on Eloquence. She expressed her admiration in a chaplet of verses which, finding their way into the orator's hands, so impressed him with the fair promise they contained, that he secured an introduction to the author. Thus originated one of Hannah's numerous warm friendships of after life.

Ferguson, the astronomer, was another of Hannah's early acquaintances. From him she gained a knowledge of science; whilst he, prompted by his high estimate of her abilities, took counsel with her respecting the style of his literary productions.

Her intellectual tastes were encouraged and directed, to a large extent, by a somewhat notable Bristol man, of the name of Peach. Although a draper by trade, his cultivated mind and excellent literary judgment were of distinct service to his young friend. He was entrusted by Hume with the revision of the proof-sheets of the famous History of England.

A humorous story is related of the interest which Hannah's conversation created in the minds of her elders. When laid aside by illness she was attended by a noted physician, Dr. Woodward, who one day became so absorbed in his patient's intellectual discourse that he forgot to make the usual inquiries about her health. "Bless me!" he exclaimed, as he went downstairs, "I forgot to ask the girl how she was!" He returned to the bedside, and rather awkwardly put the formal question to the amused invalid, "How are you today, my poor child?"

Hannah's training in the highest principles of morality and in religion, begun by her devoted parents, received the careful attention of her eldest sister as long as she remained under her care; when out of her teens, she commenced the study of theology under the guidance of Dr. Stonhouse, a clergyman of Bristol.

At the age of seventeen, finding that the young people in her circle were in the habit of learning passages from plays which frequently savored of unhealthy sentiment, she conceived the idea of providing a harmless substitute, and thereupon wrote a pastoral drama, "The Search after

Happiness." A little later she produced another drama, "The Inflexible Captive," founded on Metastasio's opera of "Regulus."

Encouraged in various ways by numerous friends, on whose judgment she could safely rely, she appears to have taken pains to qualify herself for a literary career. She studied Latin, Italian, and Spanish, translated from the best compositions, wrote pieces in imitation of celebrated authors, and thus tried to cultivate her mind, and to form the groundwork of a good and pleasing style.

Such literary prospects, however, seemed likely to be exchanged for those of a rural domestic life; for at the age of twenty-two she received and accepted an offer of marriage from a country gentleman of wealth and high character. The wedding-day was fixed, but was postponed more than once, owing to the bridegroom's indecision. At length he lost his chance; for the bride, yielding to the advice of friends, declined to be trifled with any longer, and broke off the engagement. To make some amends for his treatment, and to compensate for her resignation, at the prospect of marriage, of her interest in the school which she and her sister were conducting at Bristol, he settled upon her an annuity, and at his death bequeathed her a thousand pounds. The settlement was made without her knowledge; and it was not without the utmost difficulty that her friends prevailed in persuading her to agree to the arrangement. From this time forward she seems to have set her face against matrimony, for she firmly declined other offers.

A few years afterwards, on arriving at the age of twenty-eight, a long-cherished wish was realized. Since childhood she had longed to visit London. As a child her favorite amusement was to make a carriage of a chair, and invite her sisters to ride with her to London "to see bishops and booksellers." Through girlhood to womanhood the desire gathered strength. In 1773 she set off with two of her sisters to pay her first visit to the Metropolis.

CHAPTER II

IN "VANITY FAIR"

IN order to estimate the complex influences surrounding Hannah More in London, and to appreciate the manner in which she stood the ordeal of passing through "Vanity Fair," it is necessary to bear in mind the social, moral, and religious aspects of the people about the middle of the eighteenth century.

What are now considered flagrant vices were either un-noticed or tacitly sanctioned. Of social refinement, as we now understand the term, there was comparatively little. Coarse jokes, swearing, and profanity were almost as common in "polite society" as in the back streets now. The literature of the day, excepting the writings of Addison, Johnson, Steele, and a few others, ministered to the low tastes prevalent amongst both the upper and the lower classes. Religion had well nigh lost all vitality. With the majority of people it had become the subject either of jest, skeptical hostility, or the utmost indifference.

One of Archbishop Seeker's charges contained the fol-lowing startling statement:—"In this we cannot be mistak-en, that an open and professed disregard of religion is become, through a variety of unhappy causes, the distin-guishing character of the present age . . . Indeed, it hath already brought in such dissoluteness and contempt of

principle in the higher part of the world, and such profligate intemperance and fearlessness of committing crimes
in the lower part, as must, if this torrent of impiety stop
not, become absolutely fatal . . . Christianity is now ridi-
culed and railed at with very little reserve; and the teach-
ers of it without any at all."*

The great lawyer, Blackstone, says he went from church
to church to hear noted London preachers, and it was
impossible for him to tell from their discourses whether
these luminaries were followers of Confucius, Mahomet, or
Christ. George III felt compelled to address a letter of
expostulation to Archbishop Cornwallis for giving balls and
routs at Lambeth Palace on Saturday nights, so that they
ran into Sunday morning.† The Church had given hardly a
thought to either the religious or secular education of the
masses. Gross ignorance pervaded the ranks of the poor all
over England. Although the English Bible was in the
people's hands, it was almost a dead letter.

But the voice of awakening had been heard in the land.
George Whitfield, John Wesley, and a few other brave
men, whose hearts were roused by the Spirit of God, went
up and down the country proclaiming the glad tidings of
the cross, which for so long had been as an idle tale to the
English people.

The wave of religious awakening had touched the highest circles of London society; and when Hannah More
received her flattering welcome from fashion, wit, and
genius in 1773, the spirit of indifference and neglect had
given way in a slight degree to a spirit of inquiry and
anxious concern. There was, however, no perceptible

---

* Charge to clergy, 1738. See vol. v. of "Works," Dublin, 1775.
† This letter may be found in "The Life and Times of Lady Huntingdon."

change as yet in the utter worldliness of the times, or in the low standard of morals.

It was a perilous thing for a young woman like Hannah More, with her enthusiasm, talents, and general attractiveness, to be suddenly launched in the turbid though fascinating current of London society. But the admirable training in strict moral principles with which she had been privileged furnished weapons of defense against the more specious temptations which presented themselves; whilst her quick discernment easily penetrated the thin shell of external polish covering worthlessness of character. It was also fortunate for her that at the outset of her London experience she became acquainted with such a sterling man as Dr. Johnson.

A few days after her arrival she was introduced to David Garrick and his wife. The famous actor had seen a letter of hers to a mutual friend, extolling one of his theatrical performances. He forthwith secured an interview, which resulted in favorable impressions on both sides, of amiability and intellectual powers. A very cordial friendship ensued.

Garrick's social circle was now thrown open to Miss More. At his house she first met Mrs. Elizabeth Montague, the authoress of an "Essay on the Writings and Genius of Shakespeare," a work which brought around the writer the best literary men of the time.

Miss More's introduction to Dr. Johnson took place at the house of Sir Joshua Reynolds. This event, though much desired, was not without dread, lest the great man should happen to be in one of his querulous moods. All fear vanished on her seeing the Doctor approach with a smile on his rugged countenance, and Sir Joshua's macaw perched on his hand. Her surprise may be imagined when he greeted her with a verse from a Morning Hymn of her own composition.

The following extracts are from letters written by one of Hannah's vivacious sisters. "Since I last wrote, Hannah has been introduced by Miss Reynolds to Baretti and to Edmund Burke (the 'Sublime and Beautiful' Edmund Burke!). From a large party of literary persons assembled at Sir Joshua's she received the most encouraging compliments; and the spirit with which she returned them was acknowledged by all present, as Miss Reynolds informed poor us. Miss R. repeats her little poem by heart, with which also the great Johnson is much pleased." "We have paid another visit to Miss Reynolds. She had sent to engage Dr. Percy (Percy's collection,—now you know him), who is quite a sprightly modern, instead of a rusty antique, as I expected. He was no sooner gone, than the most amiable and obliging of women (Miss Reynolds) ordered the coach to take us to Dr. Johnson's *very own house*; yes, Abyssinia's Johnson! Dictionary Johnson! Rambler's, Idler's, and Irene's Johnson! Can you picture to yourself the palpitation of our hearts as we approached his mansion? The conversation turned upon a new work of his (the Tour to the Hebrides), and his old friend Richardson . . . Miss Reynolds told the doctor of all our rapturous exclamations on the road. He shook his scientific head at Hannah, and said, 'She was a *silly thing.*' When our visit was ended, he called for his hat, as it rained, to attend us down a very long entry to our coach, and not Rasselas could have acquitted himself more *en cavalier*. We are engaged with him at Sir Joshua's, Wednesday evening. What do you think of us?"

A second visit to London took place in the following year, and a third—prolonged to six months—in 1776. From this period down to about 1789 Miss More usually spent some time every year amongst her London friends, but chiefly with Mrs. Garrick, either at the Adelphi or at her country residence at Hampton.

Her "Life," written by Mr. Roberts and others, is rich with letters, which of themselves form a striking autobiography, revealing the writer's prominent phases of character, her steadfast adhesion to high principles, her progress in the path of literary fame, her wearying of fashionable society, and the gradual consecration of all her powers to the service of God. Besides these personal matters, we get glimpses of the notable people with whom she was brought into contact, and of the moral and religious condition of the higher classes. These letters conform to Hannah More's own idea of what epistolary effusions between friends should be. "What I want in a letter," she once wrote, "is the picture of my friend's mind, and the common course of his life. I want to know what he is saying and doing; I want him to turn out the inside of his heart to me, without disguise, without appearing better than he is." We can therefore obtain a more lifelike portraiture by making extracts from her correspondence than by attempting the task in any other way.

Describing her feelings in associating with persons of rank and wit, she says:—"I had yesterday the pleasure of dining in Hill Street, Berkeley Square, at a certain Mrs. Montague's, a name not totally obscure. The party consisted of herself, Mrs. Carter, Dr. Johnson, Solander, and Matty, Mrs. Boscawen, Miss Reynolds, and Sir Joshua (the idol of every company); some other persons of high rank and less wit, and your humble servant,—a party that would not have disgraced the table of Laelius or of Atticus. I felt myself a worm for the consequence which was given me, by mixing me with such a society; but as I told Mrs. Boscawen, and with great truth, I had an opportunity of making an experiment of my heart, by which I learnt that I was not envious, for I certainly did not repine at being the meanest person in company . . . Dr. Johnson asked me how I liked the new tragedy of Braganza. I was afraid to speak before them all, as I knew a diversity of opinion prevailed among the company: however, as I thought it less evil to dissent from the opinion of a fellow-creature than to tell a falsity, I ventured to give my sentiments, and was satisfied with Johnson's answering, 'You are right, madam.'"

Her conscience was uneasy from visiting the opera, and also from attending Sunday parties, which were greatly in vogue.

She thus wrote on this subject:—

"*London,* 1775.

" 'Bear me, some god! oh, quickly bear me hence,
    To wholesome solitude, the nurse of—'

"'Sense' I was going to add, in the words of Pope, till I recollected that *pence* had a more appropriate meaning, and was as good a rhyme. This apostrophe broke from me on coming from the opera, the first I ever *did*, the last I trust I ever *shall* go to. For what purpose has the Lord of the universe made His creature man with a comprehensive mind? Why make him a little lower than the angels? Why give him the faculty of thinking, the powers of wit and memory; and, to crown all, an immortal and never-dying spirit? Why all this wondrous waste, this prodigality of bounty, if the mere animal senses of sight and hearing (by which he is not distinguished from the brutes that perish) would have answered the end as well? and yet I find the same people are seen at the opera every night—an amusement written in a language the greater part of them do not understand, and performed by such a set of beings! . . . Conscience had done its office before; nay was busy at the time; and if it did not dash the cup of pleasure to the ground, infused at least a tincture of wormwood into it. I *did* think of the alarming call, 'What doest thou here, Elijah?' and I thought of it tonight at the opera."

The attractions of wealth and fame had not blinded her to the need of seeking satisfaction from a higher source. "For my own part, the more I see of the 'honored, famed, and great,' the more I see of the littleness, the unsatisfactoriness of all created good; and that no earthly pleasure can fill up the wants of the immortal principle within."

She was much troubled by the extravagances of fashion in dress and adornments; and, although conforming to some extent to prevailing modes in order to avoid singularity, which she abhorred, she always dressed neatly and decorously, and never, through the whole of her life, wore an article of jewelry simply for ornament.

The following extract from a letter written by one of Hannah's sisters shows the cordial relationships with Dr. Johnson, and his interest in the five sisters. "Tuesday evening we drank tea at Sir Joshua's with Dr. Johnson. Hannah is certainly a great favorite. She was placed next him, and they had the entire conversation to themselves. They were both in remarkably high spirits; it was certainly her lucky night! I never heard her say so many good things. The old genius was extremely jocular, and the young one very pleasant. You would have imagined you had been at some comedy had you heard our peals of laughter. They, indeed, tried which could 'pepper the highest,' and it is not clear to me that the lexicographer was really the highest reasoner."

CHAPTER III

CHARACTERISTICS, FRIENDSHIPS, AND EARLY LITERARY WORK

HANNAH MORE'S flattering reception in London society, and the lively impression which she so quickly created, will give rise to some astonishment in the minds of many readers. She had not yet won reputation as an authoress; she did not possess the influence of wealth or of noble family; she was not remarkable for physical beauty; and she had none of the brazen ingenuity of patronage-hunters, by which admission is secured into the houses of distinguished people. She came to London a stranger, a plain schoolmistress from Bristol, and yet in a marvellously short time she was one of the best known characters in the ranks of the wise and great.

The causes of her rapid rise to distinction are not far to seek. Her wonderful talent for conversation at once proved an attraction to both men and women. But she was not merely a fluent talker, never at a loss for a word, a phrase or a metaphor; had this been her crowning recommendation, Dr. Johnson's long-standing friendship would never have been gained. Her talk was always sensible—the outcome of a well-furnished, retentive mind. Her judgment was sound, her discrimination delicate, and her grasp of fundamental truths consistently firm. She did not accommodate her opinions to meet the exigencies of different coteries, nor was she addicted to compromise. She was equally at ease in discussing the merits of *Rasselas* with Dr. Johnson, the curiosities of art with Lord Orford, Roman history with Gibbon, and the state of the Church with Bishop Porteus. Not that she pretended equality of learning with such men, but she had just sufficient knowledge of various subjects to provoke a conversation, and enough cleverness to sustain it by "drawing out" the scholar who might be seated at her side. But this was not all. Her conversation sparkled with wit and repartee. "The mind laughed," says her friend Zachary Macaulay, "not the muscles; the countenance sparkled, but it was with an ethereal flame: everything was oxygen gas and intellectual champagne: and the eye, which her sisters called 'diamond,' and which the painters complained they could not put upon canvas, often gave signal by its coruscation, as the same sort of eye did in her friend Mr. Wilberforce, that something was forthcoming which in a less amiable and religiously disciplined mind might have been very pretty satire, but which glanced off innoxiously in the shape of epigrammatic playfulness."

Her genial disposition and good temper disarmed differ-ence of opinion of anything harsh or unpleasant, and formed another credential for the prominence she attained in society. The absence of all artificiality in sentiment and manners, when contrasted with the straining after effect acquired by fashionably-bred ladies, also added to her attractions in the eyes of thoughtful men.

But whilst to these causes may be attributed her rapid rise into favor, it was undoubtedly owing to her unswerving and unassuming piety that she retained for so long the respect, confidence, and affection of varied orders of mind in London society.

At first she appears to have done little to enforce religious teaching amongst her acquaintances. Her moral and religious principles were known by the firm stand she took against common incentives to dissipation and irreligion—such as card-playing and Sunday entertainments—against the introduction of questionable topics, unseemly language, and vacuous frivolity into conversation. Her religious influence, thus far, was almost a silent or negative one; but it had its effect on others, and laid the foundation of that direct searching and far-reaching influence, which, under the Divine blessing, she wielded in later years.

Her interest in young people was notably illustrated by her efforts to foster the intellectual tastes of Lord Macaulay when a lad. She supplied him with standard books, which formed the nucleus of an excellent library, and advised him in his studies. To the child of six she thus writes:—"Though you are a little boy now, you will one day, if it please God, be a man; but long before you are a man I hope you will be a scholar."*

When Hannah More began to produce books her reputation rose to literary fame. In 1775 she wrote a romantic poem, entitled "Sir Eldred of the Bouer," with which was published another poem, written earlier, "The Bleeding Rock." In the first the element of religion was not forgotten; and both works met with a flattering reception. Though, as we have seen, a woman of high Christian tone, with what we should consider strange inconsistency, she both wrote plays, which were acted, and attended the theatre herself.

---

* See "Life and Letters of Lord Macaulay," by George Otto Trevelyan, M.P., vol. 1. pp. 35, 36.

In 1777 her tragedy, "Percy," was brought out at Covent Garden Theatre. One of the results of this venture was a shower of invitations to the author of the play from a new circle of titled and distinguished people. The play was afterwards translated into German, and performed at Vienna with notable success.

On the death of Garrick in 1779, Hannah More broke off attendance at the theatre. Garrick's widow sought relief and solace in Hannah's company, and for many years a close friendship was kept up between the two ladies, although there could be but little intercourse on religious matters, Mrs. Garrick being a Roman Catholic. Before the actor's death Miss More had completed another play, "The Fatal Falsehood," which was afterwards performed, and which elicited almost as much applause as "Percy."

Miss More's experience of fashionable life had now lasted about six years. As her fame increased, her taste for society declined. The constant round of dinner-parties, conversation-parties, and assemblies of intellect and wealth, though at first full of attraction to one of her disposition, had begun to lose its charm. Her depth of character and her recognition of the claims of religion demanded a more satisfactory mode of spending her time and utilizing her talents. For the next five years we find her often the guest of Mrs. Garrick, but gradually detaching herself from fashionable circles, studying theology, history, and science, writing poems, and engaged in other literary work.

Her chief literary work during this period consisted of "Sacred Dramas—Moses in the Bulrushes, David and Goliath, Belshazzar," and "Daniel." She was prompted to this undertaking by a desire to provide, not plays for the stage, but a substitute for some of the pernicious literature of the day which fell into the hands of young people, and also to afford instruction in the common facts of Scripture. The gross ignorance of the Bible amongst fashionable people astonished her one day, when Sir Joshua Reynolds told her that on showing his picture of Samuel to some great patrons they asked him who Samuel was? The work answered the purpose for which it was intended, and passed through nineteen editions, receiving high commendation from Bishop Lowth and others. Her poem "Sensibility" was also included in this successful volume.

A poem, "The Bas Bleu, or Conversation," written in a lively and facetious strain, owed its origin to the mistakes of a foreigner who gave the literal designation of the "Bas Bleu" to a party of friends who had been humorously called the "Blue Stockings."

At the King's request a manuscript copy of the poem was sent to him; and Dr. Johnson went so far in his praise of the effusion as to say that there was no name in poetry that might not be glad to own it. A little later Miss More wrote "Florio," a poem describing the occupation of a young man of fashion, and his final escape from a life of pleasure to one of usefulness.

By the death of Dr. Johnson in 1784, Miss More lost the best friend she ever had in London. She had been with the Doctor at his last communion at St. Clement's Church, and saw too plainly his altered condition. Bound to each other by strong intellectual and stronger religious sympathies, the separation caused a void in Miss More's life which was never afterwards filled. Theirs was a friendship born at first sight. For more than ten years it grew and flourished, with mutual benefit and happiness to the stern moralist and his promising *protégé*. Whilst the rugged common-sense and sound literary judgments of the Doctor imparted increasing accuracy and insight to his friend's views of the world and of literature, it was the sparkle, freshness, and wit of Miss More's conversation, and her light-heartedness of character, that often dispelled the clouds of depression from the mental horizon of her sage and trusty adviser, and smoothed the rough edges of his outspoken opinions. In religion, it was probably the Doctor's uncompromising fidelity to first principles, and to a fearless practice of truth, that helped to fortify his "dear child," as he called Miss More, in maintaining her integrity amidst the bewildering voices and garish scenes of Vanity Fair.

CHAPTER IV

COWSLIP GREEN

ABOUT the time of Dr. Johnson's death, in 1784, Hannah More became the possessor of a rural spot, called Cowslip Green, some ten miles from Bristol. Here she built herself a cottage, intending to make it her place of retirement for a large portion of each year. In the cultivation of her garden she found leisure for reflection as well as an opportunity to pursue a favorite occupation.

The inroads which death had made in her circle of intimate friends, a growing dissatisfaction with the enjoyments of London life, and especially a keener sense of her responsibility, as a professed Christian, than she had hitherto experienced, led to a close self-examination, and to a scrutiny of the real motives of her life.

The result of this testing process showed itself in various ways. During occasional visits to London and attendance at parties she lost no opportunity of enforcing the truths of religion. Her silent witnessing was now exchanged for active exertion. The manners and practices of people who were amongst her most effusive admirers sometimes met with her indignant rebuke. Ladies of title, society beauties, and leaders of fashion, who were unapproachable by other religious influences, she urged in private to consider their spiritual interests. The method she adopted was not, usually, to start religious topics, but "to extract from common subjects some useful and awful truth, and to counteract the mischief of a popular senti-ment by one drawn from religion." Perhaps a message which John Wesley once sent to her through a sister may have weighed considerably in deterring her from an entire severance from the fashionable world. "Tell her to live in the world; *there* is the sphere of her usefulness; they will not let *us* come nigh them."

Not content with personal and private reproof, advice, and entreaty, she now devoted her pen to the denunciation of folly and vice in high places. In her work, "Thoughts on the Importance of the Manners of the Great to General Society," whilst protesting against prevalent irreligious practices and habits of dissipation, which even good people sanctioned, she sought to arouse a sensitive regard for mutual responsibility as set forth in the New Testament.

In 1788 the slave trade formed a burning question in Parliament. Miss More, intensely aroused by the descrip-tions presented of the horrible traffic, found vent for her feelings in a poem on the subject. About the same time a close friendship began with Wilberforce, which lasted to the end of life.

A yet more important friendship commenced at this period—one that was destined to work a powerful influence on Miss More's life. The Rev. John Newton, one of the leaders amongst the evangelical clergy, held the incumbency of St. Mary Woolnoth. Attendance on his ministry led to a correspondence and a deep friendship. John Newton was precisely the kind of man whom Hannah More needed to assist her in spiritual progress, and to direct her steps into paths of settled peace. Her letters to Mr. Newton, stating her difficulties and seeking counsel, breathe the spirit of the humble and sincere scholar of Christ. Her willingness to obey the Master whom she professed to serve, and her earnest desire to be brought into closer relations with God, although checked, had never been stifled by the claims of intellect or by the attractions of the world. From this time the work of the Holy Spirit in deepening her love for the Savior became more and more prominent. Turning for a time from Christian work amongst the rich, Miss More now devoted her efforts to the improvement of the moral and religious condition of the poor.

About ten miles from Cowslip Green was the picturesque village of Cheddar, the population of which was sunk in ignorance and depravity. The incumbent lived at Oxford, and the curate at Wells, twelve miles off. There was but one service a week, and no pastoral visitation whatever. There were thirteen parishes in the neighborhood without even a resident curate. Drunkenness and utter inefficiency prevailed to a terrible extent amongst the clergy in this district; whilst education was a question that never troubled either the clergy or the people.

At Cheddar Hannah and her sister Patty opened a school; and in a short time nearly 300 children attended regularly. The sisters had to combat strong prejudices amongst the farmers. By dint of much persuasion and flattery the opposing forces were at length won over, even to hearty concurrence.

Masters and mistresses were procured for teaching reading, seeing, knitting, and spinning, and giving religious instruction on Sundays. A second school was shortly opened in an adjoining parish, the vicarage-house, which had remained uninhabited for a hundred years, having been put into repair for the purpose.

During 1790 Miss More published a volume entitled, "An Estimate of the Religion of the Fashionable World." The book was quickly bought up, and within two years reached a fifth edition. The prevailing indifference to vital religion, the corruptions of society, the decline of domestic piety, and the absence of religion from the education of the upper classes were the themes treated by the writer with unsparing candor and convincing force.

Encouraged by her success at Cheddar, Miss More, with her sister Patty, went further afield, and selected two mining villages on the top of the Mendip Hills as the next scene of her labors. The difficulties here were even greater than those at Cheddar. The neighborhood was so bad, we are told, that no constable would venture to execute his office there. Friends warned the Misses More that their lives would be in danger if they persisted in their project. The people imagined that the sisters had come to make money by kidnapping their children for slaves.

Undaunted by obstacles and perils, the workers perse-vered, until in no less than ten parishes schools were commenced, which, before long, were attended by 1200 children. In every parish the acquiescence of the incum-bent was first obtained before proceeding to open a school. At the evening meetings, to which adults were invited, a simple sermon was read by one of the sisters, and also a printed prayer and a psalm. Few mistresses could be found who had not owed their religious impressions to Wesleyan influence; and thus Hannah More was subsequently, though mistakenly, thought to be a Methodist. Although influenced by the Methodist revival, she always considered and professed herself to be a member of the Episcopal Church.

Whilst immersed in her village work, she was earnestly solicited to write a popular tract that might help to counteract the baneful influence of Jacobin and infidel publications, and infamous ballads, which were now scattered broadcast over England. She declined the task, doubtful of her efficiency to produce a pamphlet equal to the occasion. On second thoughts, however, she tried her powers in secret, and issued anonymously a lively dialogue called "Village Politics," by "Will Chip." The success was phenomenal. Friends ignorant of the authorship sent her copies by every post within three or four days of publication, begging her to distribute the pamphlet as widely as possible. In a short time copies were to be found in all parts of the kingdom. Hundreds of thousands were circulated in London. Such was the enthusiasm that private persons printed large editions at their own expense, whilst the Government sent off quantities to Scotland and Ireland. At last the secret came out; and the author was deluged with congratulations and thanks. Some persons of sound judgment declared that "Village Politic" had essentially contributed, under Providence, to prevent a revolution, whilst others went so far as to allege that Miss More had "wielded at will the fierce démocratie of England, and stemmed the tide of misguided opinion."

A little later Miss More wrote another pamphlet, by way of reply to the atheistical speech of Dupont to the National

Convention, and devoted the profits, amounting to £240, towards the relief of the French emigrant clergy.

In 1794, or early in 1795, she commenced the issue of tracts. This was a form of literary work not much used in those days. The founders of the Religious Tract Society, realizing the value of this kind of work, but considering that Miss More's tracts needed supplementing with some which should in every case contain the simple communication of the Gospel, began in 1799 to undertake the dissemination of religious knowledge. Sunday schools, through the energy of Mr. Raikes, were rising in various parts of the country; the poorer classes were learning to read; and nothing in the shape of cheap literature was provided to meet their new craving, except mischievous broadsheets and worthless doggerel. Hannah More set to work to supply something healthy to amuse, instruct, and edify the new order of readers. She produced regularly every month for three years, three tracts—simple, pithy, vivacious, consisting of stories, ballads, homilies, and prayers. She was sometimes assisted by one of her sisters and two or three friends; but the burden of the work, including heavy correspondence with local committees in almost every district of England, fell upon her shoulders. In order to issue the brochures at a cheap rate and to undersell pernicious publications, she found it necessary to raise a subscription. Her appeal met with a liberal response; and very shortly the lively tracts, with a rough woodcut on the title-page, came by thousands from the printer's hands. In the first year no less than two millions were sold. Amongst the tracts were "The Shepherd of Salisbury Plain, Black Giles the Poacher, History of Mr. Fantom, The Two Shoemakers,

History of Tom White the Postilion, The Strait Gate and
the Broad Way;" and amongst the ballads "Turning the
Carpet, King Dionysius and Squire Damocles, The Honest
Miller of Gloucestershire, The Gin-Shop, or A Peep into a
Prison."

It would be difficult to over-estimate both the direct and
secondary value of the Cheap Repository Tracts. Their
beneficial influence must have been incalculable; and for
this reason they should be placed amongst the greatest
and best work of Hannah More's useful life.

By 1798 Miss More had withdrawn almost entirely from
London society, contenting herself with a yearly visit of
two months, which she divided between Mrs. Garrick,
Bishop Porteus, Lord Teignmouth, and one or two others.
Her schools occupied the best part of her time; but fre-
quent attacks of illness often interfered with her duties.

In 1799 her active pen was at work again. Her third eth-
ical publication, "Strictures on Female Education," came
out, forming yet another counterblast to the corrupt sys-
tems in vogue amongst the wealthy classes.

It would have been marvelous had Miss More escaped
persecution in her work amongst rural populations. Combat-
ing prejudices, introducing unheard of innovations, adopting
plans which rumor stated were deeply tainted with Method-
ism (and therefore bad, according to clerical and general
opinion in those days), she had to encounter at last a pitiless
storm of hostility. This violent and prolonged attack, whilst it
showed to what infamous lengths the tongues of slander,
envy, and bigotry could go in attempting to destroy a noble
woman's reputation, tested to the utmost Hannah More's
fine qualities of Christian forbearance and courage.

CHAPTER V

BARLEY WOOD, CLOSING YEARS AND DEATH

IN 1802 Miss More removed from Cowslip Green to a house which she had built at Barley Wood, about a mile distant. Soon afterwards her sisters, having disposed of their house at Bath, came to live with her. For the next twenty years, or more, friends from all parts sought her society, and strangers of all ages and of all ranks came for advice, sympathy, and help. Her immense correspondence occupied a very large portion of her time. There was scarcely a person at all prominent in the religious world who was not brought into association with her.

Miss More's prolonged life did not close until 1833, when she had arrived at her eighty-ninth year. The thirty-one years that remained to her after quitting Cowslip Green was as full of work and usefulness as the previous part of her life. It will be impossible within the space now left to do more than indicate the chief events of this period, which was not remarkable for any fresh departure either in educational or religious work. Miss More had already marked out for herself two distinct and definite lines of usefulness—the education of the poor, and the improvement of morals and religion amongst the rich. By her active exertion and by her busy pen she continued to pursue these two lines of work down to the year of her death. It must be remembered that she was a martyr during these latter years to long attacks of illness, one of which almost completely prostrated her for two years; and when upwards of seventy she was unable to leave the house for more than seven years. At this period she stated that she had never been free from pain for long together since she was ten years old. Such physical hindrances render her persistent activity and the great work she accomplished all the more remarkable. When not entirely incapacitated she still worked with her pen, attended to business connected with her schools, and received visitors in the sick room. It used to be said amongst her friends that when she was laid aside they always expected a new book from her.

In 1805 she published "Hints Towards Forming the Character of a Young Princess." It was undertaken, at the request of a bishop, with reference to the education of the Princess Charlotte.

In 1809 her religious novel, "Coelebs in Search of a Wife," issued anonymously, roused universal attention. In twelve months as many editions came out; and during the author's lifetime thirty editions of a thousand copies each were printed in America. This was followed shortly by "Practical Piety," which soon ran to the tenth edition, and which brought the author to the end of her life numerous gratifying testimonies of its results. As a sequel to this work, "Christian Morals" was published in 1812, and was also widely circulated. Three years later, when the author had entered her seventieth year, she wrote an "Essay on the Character and Writings of St. Paul," in two volumes, which, notwithstanding absorbing political events, was received with the same eagerness which greeted her former works.

"Moral Sketches of Prevailing Opinions and Manners, Foreign and Domestic," was published in 1819, being chiefly directed against the rage for copying French customs and manners. At the age of eighty-two she collected from her later works her "Thoughts on Prayer" and re-issued them in a little volume, with a short preface. This was her last literary effort. She said to a friend that the only remarkable thing which belonged to her as an author was that she had written eleven volumes after the age of sixty.

Between 1813 and 1818 her four sisters died. The last to go was Martha, Hannah's trusty helpmeet and lieutenant in all her benevolent schemes, and her tender consoler in many a season of sickness. Soon after this event Miss More's long illness of seven years occurred. Unable to give proper supervision to her servants, she was victimized in household matters in various ways. Extravagance and misconduct at length gave rise to scandal; and at the representation of friends Miss More reluctantly decided to break up her establishment, and remove to another and smaller residence at Clifton. It was with a sad heart that she left her charming dwelling; and as she glanced back into the beautiful garden, with its shady bowers, she exclaimed, "I am driven, like Eve, out of Paradise; but not, like Eve, by angels."

She lived five and a half years at Clifton, tranquilly waiting for the end, and attending, as far as failing strength would permit, to the distribution of her charities, the work of her schools and the entertainment of friends.

Almost to the last she retained unimpaired the use of her faculties. The intellectual vivacity of early days often reappeared. During one of her illnesses some one remarked, in allusion to the struggle of the remnant of sin in a person recently awakened to the truth, "The old man dies hard!" "The old woman dies hard!" exclaimed the invalid. At eighty-three she said, "I have too many petty cares at that age when the grasshopper is a burden. I have *many* grasshoppers, and seem to have less time and more labor than ever."

Her last days were spent almost entirely in prayer, invoking blessings on those around her and on the village work which lay so near her heart. She said to a friend during her last illness, "To go to heaven, think what *that* is! to go to my Savior who died that I might live! Lord, humble me, subdue every evil temper in me. May we meet in a robe of glory! Through Christ's merits alone can we be saved . . . Lord, I believe—I *do* believe with all the powers of my weak, sinful heart. Lord Jesus, look down upon me from Thy holy habitation; strengthen my faith, and quicken me in my preparation. Support me in that trying hour when I most need it! It is a glorious thing to die!" No vanity or self-praise on the ground of her life's labors ever found a place in her thoughts. Some one began to speak of her good deeds. "Talk not so vainly," she exclaimed; "I utterly cast them from me, and fall low at the foot of the cross." She sank gradually, and without pain, and on September 7, 1833, quietly passed away.

There are few thoughtful students who will hesitate to rank Hannah More with the leading religious and educational reformers of the eighteenth century. In essential matters she was a kindred spirit with Whitfield, Wesley, Raikes, and others, and worked, in the way marked out for her by God, for the regeneration of her country.

With regard to her books, she believed they would be little read after her death. To a considerable extent her judgment has been verified. Her writings were a continual seed-sowing, which later workers fertilized, and brought to maturity.

They were republished in eleven volumes in 1830. Besides the prominence given to their religious or moral purpose, most of them are remarkable for sustained fervor, persuasiveness of tone, and practical common sense. We give a few extracts from some of the principal works, to illustrate Hannah More's methods of appealing to the conscience and awakening spiritual concern.

"There are two things of which a wise man will be scrupulously careful—his conscience and his credit. Happily, they are almost inseparable concomitants; they are commonly kept or lost together; the same things which wound the one usually giving a blow to the other; yet it must be confessed, that conscience and a mere worldly credit are not, in all instances, allowed to subsist together . . . .

"Between a wounded conscience and a wounded credit, there is the same difference as between a crime and a calamity. Of two inevitable evils, religion instructs us to submit to that which is inferior and involuntary. As much as reputation exceeds every worldly good, so much, and far more, is conscience to be consulted before credit—if credit that can be called, which is derived from the acclamations of a mob, whether composed of 'the great vulgar or the small' "—"Christian Morals" (Chapter XXIV.).

"One cause, therefore, of the dullness of many Christians in prayer, is their slight acquaintance with the sacred volume. They hear it periodically, they read it occasionally, they are contented to know it historically, to consider it superficially; but they do not endeavor to get their minds imbued with its spirit. If they store their memory with its facts, they do not impress their hearts with its truths. They do not regard it as the nutriment on which their spiritual life and growth depend. They do not pray over it; they do not consider all its doctrines as of practical application; they do not cultivate that spiritual discernment which alone can enable them judiciously to appropriate its promises, and apply its denunciations to their own actual case. They do not use it as an unerring line, to ascertain their own rectitude, or detect their own obliquities."

"The discrepancies between our prayers and our practice do not end here. How frequently are we solemnly imploring of God that 'His kingdom may come,' while we are doing nothing to promote His kingdom of grace here, and consequently His kingdom of glory hereafter."

"Prayer draws all the Christian graces into its focus. It draws Charity, followed by her lovely train, her forbearance with faults, her forgiveness of injuries, her pity for errors, her compassion for want. It draws Repentance, with her holy sorrows, her pious resolutions, her self-distrust. It attracts Faith, with her elevated eye,—Hope, with her grasped anchor,—Beneficence, with her open hand,—Zeal, looking far and wide to serve,—Humility, with introverted eye, looking at home. Prayer, by quickening these graces in the heart warms them into life, fits them for service, and dismisses each to its appropriate practice. Cordial prayer is mental virtue; Christian virtue is spiritual action."—"The Spirit of Prayer" (Chapters III., VIII., and XI.).

Excerpted from "THE SEARCH AFTER HAPPINESS"—

"If good we plant not, vice will fill the place,
And rankest weeds the richest soils deface.
Learn how ungoverned thoughts the mind pervert,
And to disease all nourishment convert.
Ah! happy she, whose wisdom learns to find
A healthful fancy, and a well-trained mind.
A sick man's wildest dreams less wild are found
Than the day-visions of a mind unsound.
Disordered phantasies indulged too much.
Like harpies, always taint whate'er they touch.
Fly soothing Solitude! fly vain Desire!
Fly such soft verse as fans the dang'rous fire!
Seek action; 'tis the scene which virtue loves;
The vig'rous sun not only shines, but moves.
From sickly thoughts with quick abhorrence start,
And rule the fancy if you'd rule the heart:
By active goodness, by laborious schemes,
Subdue wild visions and delusive dreams.
No earthly good a Christian's views should bound,
For ever rising should his aims be found.
Leave that fictitious good your fancy feigns,
For scenes where real bliss eternal reigns:
Look to that region of immortal joys,
Where fear disturbs not, nor possession cloys;
Beyond what fancy forms of rosy bowers,
Or blooming chaplets of unfading flowers;
Fairer than o'er imagination drew,
Or poet's warmest visions ever knew.
Press eager onward to these blissful plains,
Where life eternal, joy perpetual reigns."

THE

SHEPHERD

OF

SALISBURY PLAIN*

PART I

M R. JOHNSON, a very worthy, charitable gentleman, was travelling some time ago across one of those vast plains, which are well known in Wiltshire. It was a fine summer's evening, and he rode slowly, that he might have leisure to admire God in the works of his creation. For this gentleman was of opinion, that a walk or a ride was as proper a time as any to think about good things; for which reason, on such occasions, he seldom thought so much about his money or his trade, or public news, as at other times, that he might with more ease and satisfaction enjoy the pious thoughts which the visible works of the great Maker of heaven and earth are intended to raise in the mind.

As this serene contemplation of the visible heavens insensibly lifted up his mind from the works of God in nature to the same God as he is seen in revelation, it occurred to him, that this very connection was clearly intimated by the

---

* This is not a fictitious character. The extraordinary person whose edifying history is here given, was David Sanders, a poor shepherd of West Lavington. He used to keep his Bible in the thatch of his hut, on Salisbury Plain; by reading which, and prayer, he seemed to keep up a constant communion with God. When the late Mr. Stedman of Shrewsbury went, in 1771, to settle on the curacy at Little Cheverel, the next village to Lavington, the first person he met was this shepherd, who told him, some time after, that taking the stranger to be the minister expected there, he repeated to himself those words of St. Paul, Romans 10:15, "How beautiful are the feet of them that preach the gospel of peace, and bring glad tidings of good things!"

royal prophet in nineteenth psalm,—that most beautiful description of the greatness and power of God exhibited in the former part, plainly seeming tended to introduce, illustrate, and unfold, the operations of the word and the Spirit of God on the heart on the latter. And he began to run a parallel in his own mind, between the effects of that highly poetical and glowing picture of the material sun in searching and warming the earth, in the first six verses, and the spiritual opera attributed to the "law of God," which fills up the remaining part of the psalm. And he persuaded himself the divine Spirit which dictated this fine hymn, had left it as a kind of a general intimation to what use we were to convert our admiration of created things; namely, that we might be led by a sight of them to raise our views from the kingdom of nature to that of grace, and that the contemplation of God in his works might draw us to contemplate him in his word.

In the midst of these reflections, Mr. Johnson's attention was all of a sudden called off by the barking of a shepherd's dog, and looking up, he spied one of those little huts, which are here and there to be seen on those great downs; and near it was the shepherd himself, busily employed with his dog in collecting together his vast flock of sheep. As he drew nearer, he perceived him to be a clean, well-looking poor man, near fifty years of age. His coat, though at first it had probably been of one dark color, had been in a long course of years, so often patched with different sorts of cloth, that it had now become hard to say which had been the original color. But this, while it gave plain proof of the shepherd's poverty, equally proved the exceeding neatness, industry, and good management of his wife.

His stockings no less proved her good housewifery, for they were entirely covered with darns of different colored worsted, but had not a hole in them; and his shirt, though nearly as coarse as the sails of a ship, was as white as the drifted snow, and was neatly mended where time had either made a rent* or worn it thin.

This furnishes a rule of judging, by which one will seldom be deceived. If I meet with a laborer hedging, ditching, or mending the highways, with his stockings and shirt tight and whole, however mean and bad his other garments are, I have seldom failed, on visiting his cottage, to find that also clean and well-ordered, and his wife notable, and worthy of encouragement. Whereas a poor woman who will be lying abed,† or gossiping with her neighbors, when she ought to be fitting out her husband in a cleanly manner, will seldom be found to be very good in other respects.

This was not the case with our shepherd; and Mr. Johnson was not more struck with the decency of his mean and frugal dress, than with his open, honest countenance, which bore strong marks of health, cheerfulness, and spirit.

Mr. Johnson, who was on a journey, and somewhat fearful from the appearance of the sky, that rain was at no great distance, accosted the shepherd with asking what sort of weather he thought it would be on the morrow.

"It will be such weather as pleases me," answered the shepherd.

Though the answer was delivered in the mildest and civilest tone that could be imagined, the gentleman thought the words themselves rather rude and surly, and asked him how that could be.

---

* Rent—a tear.
† Abed—in bed.

MR. JOHNSON MEETS THE SHEPHERD.

"Because," replied the shepherd, "it will be such weather as shall please God, and whatever pleases him, always pleases me."

Mr. Johnson, who delighted in good men and good things, was very well satisfied with his reply. For he justly thought, that though a hypocrite may easily contrive to appear better than he really is to a stranger, and that no one should be too soon trusted, merely for having a few good words in his mouth; yet, as he knew that "out of the abundance of the heart the mouth speaketh,"* he always accustomed himself to judge favorably of those who had a serious deportment and solid manner of speaking. "It looks as if it proceeded from a good habit," said he, "and though I may now and then be deceived by it, yet it has not often happened to me to be so. Whereas, if a man accosts me with an idle, disso-lute, vulgar, indecent, or profane expression, I have never been deceived in him, but have generally on inquiry, found his character to be as bad as his language gave me room to expect."

He entered into conversation with the shepherd in the following manner: "Yours is a troublesome life, honest friend," said he.

"To be sure, sir," replied the shepherd, "'tis not a very lazy life; but 'tis not near so toilsome as that which my GREAT MASTER led for my sake; and he had every state and condition of life at his choice, and *chose* a hard one, while I only submit to the lot that is appointed me."

"You are exposed to great cold and heat," said the gentleman.

---

* Luke 6:45—A good man out of the good treasure of his heart bringeth forth that which is good; and an evil man out of the evil treasure of his heart bringeth forth that which is evil: for of the abundance of the heart his mouth speaketh.

"True, sir," said the shepherd, "but then I am not exposed to great temptations; and so throwing one thing against another, God is pleased to contrive to make things more equal than we poor, ignorant, short-sighted creatures are apt to think. David was happier when he kept his father's sheep on such a plain as this, and was employed in singing some of his own psalms, perhaps, than ever he was when he became king of Israel and Judah. And I dare say we should never have had some of the most beautiful texts in all those fine psalms, if he had not been a shepherd, which enabled him to make so many fine comparisons and similitudes, as one may say, from country life, flocks of sheep, hills and valleys, and fountains of water."

"You think, then," said the gentleman, "that a laborious life is a happy one."

"I do, sir; and more so especially as it exposes a man to fewer sins. If King Saul had continued a poor, laborious man to the end of his days, he might have lived happy and honest, and died a natural death in his bed at last, which you know, sir, was more than he did. But I speak with reverence; for it was Divine Providence overruled all that, you know, sir, and I do not presume to make comparisons. Besides, sir, my employment has been particularly honored. Moses was a shepherd in the plains of Midian. It was to 'shepherds keeping their flocks by night,'* that the angels appeared in Bethlehem, to tell the best news, the gladdest tidings, that ever were revealed to poor sinful men; often and often has the thought warmed my poor heart in the coldest night, and filled me with more joy and thankfulness than the best supper could have done."

---

* Luke 2:8—And there were in the same country shepherds abiding in the field, keeping watch over their flock by night.

Here the shepherd stopped, for he began to feel that he had made too free, and had talked too long. But Mr. Johnson was so well pleased with what he said, and with the cheerful, contented manner in which he said it, that he desired him to go on freely, for it was a pleasure to him to meet with a plain man, who, without any kind of learning but what he had got from the Bible, was able to talk so well on a subject which all men, high and low, rich and poor, are equally concerned.

"Indeed, I am afraid I make too bold, sir, for it better becomes me to listen to such a gentleman as you seem to be, than to talk in my poor way; but as I was saying, sir, I wonder all working men do not derive as great joy and delight as I do from thinking how God has honored poverty! O, sir, what great, or rich, or mighty men have had such honor put on them or their condition, as shepherds, tent-makers, fishermen, and carpenters have had? Besides, it seems as if God honored industry also. The way of duty is not only the way of safety, but it is remarkable how many, in the exercise of the common duties of their calling, humbly and rightly performed, as we may suppose, have found honors, preferment, and blessing; while it does not occur to me, that the whole sacred volume presents a single instance of a like blessing conferred on idleness. Rebekah, Rachel, and Jethro's daughters, were diligently employed in the lowest occupations of a country life, when Providence, by means of those very occupations, raised them up husbands so famous in history as Isaac, Jacob, and the prophet Moses. The shepherds were neither playing nor sleeping, but 'watching their flocks,' when they received the news of a Savior's birth; and the woman of

Samaria, by the laborious office of drawing water, was brought to the knowledge of Him who gave her to drink of 'living water.'"

"My honest friend," said the gentleman, "I perceive you are well acquainted with Scripture."

"Yes, sir, pretty well, blessed be God! Through his mercy I learned to read when I was a little boy; though reading was not so common when I was a child, as I am told, through the goodness of Providence, and the generosity of the rich, it is likely to become nowadays. I believe there is no day for the last thirty years, that I have not peeped at my Bible. If we can't find time to read a chapter, I defy any man to say he can't find time to read a verse; and a single text, sir, well followed and put in practice every day, would make no bad figure at the year's end; three hundred and sixty-five texts; without the loss of a moment's time, would make a pretty stock, a little golden treasury, as one may say, from New-Year's Day to New-Year's Day; and if children were brought up to it, they would come to look for their texts as naturally as they do for their breakfast.

"No laboring man, 'tis true, has so much leisure as a shepherd; for while the flock is feeding, I am obliged to be still, and at such times I can now and then tap a shoe for my children or myself, which is a great saving to us; and while I am doing that, I repeat a bit of a chapter or a psalm, which makes the time pass pleasantly in this wild, solitary place. I can say the best part of the New Testament by heart; I believe I should not say the best part, for every part is good; but I mean the greatest part. I have led but a lonely life, and have often had but little to eat; but my

Bible has been meat, drink, and company to me, as I may say; and when want and trouble have come upon me, I don't know what I should have done indeed, sir, if I had not had the promises of this book for my stay and support."

"You have had great difficulties, then?" said Mr. Johnson.

"Why, as to that, sir, not more than neighbors' fare; I have but little cause to complain, and much to be thankful; but I have had some little struggles, as I will leave you to judge. I have a wife and eight children, whom I bred up in that little cottage which you see under the hill about half a mile off."

"What, that with the smoke coming out of the chimney?" said the gentleman.

"O no, sir," replied the shepherd, smiling, "we have seldom smoke in the evening, for we have little to cook, and firing is very dear in these parts. 'Tis that cottage which you see on the left hand of the church, near that little tuft of hawthorns."

"What, that hovel with only one room above and below, with scarcely any chimney? How is it possible you can live there with such a family?"

"O, it is very possible, and very certain too," cried the shepherd. "How many better men have been worse lodged; how many good Christians have perished in prisons and dungeons, in comparison of which my cottage is a palace. The house is very well, sir, and if the rain did not sometimes beat down upon us through the thatch when we are abed, I should not desire a better; for I have health, peace, and liberty, and no man maketh me afraid."

"Well, I will certainly call upon you before it be long; but how can you contrive to lodge so many children?"

"We do the best we can, sir. My poor wife is a very sickly woman, or we should always have done tolerably well. There are no gentry in the parish, so that she has not met with any great assistance in her sickness. The good curate of the parish, who lives in that pretty parsonage in the valley, is very willing, but not very able to assist us on these trying occasions, for he has little enough for himself, and a large family into the bargain. Yet he does what he can, and more than many richer men do, and more than he can well afford. Besides that, his prayers and good advice we are always sure of, and we are truly thankful for that; for a man must give, you know, sir, according to what he hath, and not according to what he hath not."

"I am afraid," said Mr. Johnson, "that your difficulties may sometimes lead you to repine."

"No, sir," replied the shepherd; "it pleases God to give me two ways of bearing up under them. I pray that they may be either removed or sanctified to me. Besides, if my road be right, I am contented, though it be rough and uneven. I do not so much stagger at hardships in the right way, as I dread a false security and a hollow peace, while I may be walking in a more smooth but less safe way. Besides, sir, I strengthen my faith by recollecting what the best men have suffered and my hope with the view of the shortness of all suffering. It is a good hint, sir, of the vanity of all earthly possessions and though the whole land of promise was his, yet the first bit of ground which Abraham, the father of the faithful, got possession of, in the land of Canaan, was a *grave*."

"Are you in any distress at present?" said Mr. Johnson.

"No, sir, thank God," replied the shepherd. "I get my shilling a day, and most of my children will soon be able to earn something; for we have only three under five years old."

"Only!" said the gentleman; "that is a heavy burden."

"Not at all; God fits the back to it. Though my wife is not able to do any out-of-door work, yet she breeds up her children to such habits of industry, that our little maids, before they are six years old, can first get a half-penny, and then a penny a day, by knitting. The boys who are too little to do hard work, get a trifle by keeping the birds off the corn; for this the farmers will give them a penny or twopence, and now and then a bit of bread and cheese into the bargain. When the season of crow-keeping is over, then they glean or pick stones; any thing is better than idleness, sir; and if they did not get a farthing by it, I would make them do it just the same, for the sake of giving them early habits of labor.

"So you see, sir, I am not so badly off as many are: nay, if it were not that it cost me so much in 'potecary's* stuff for my poor wife, I should reckon myself well off; nay, I do reckon myself well off, for, blessed be God, he has granted her life to my prayers, and I would work myself to a 'nato‑my,† and live on one meal a day, to add one comfort to her valuable life; indeed, I have often done the last, and thought it no great matter neither."

While they were in this part of the discourse, a fine, plump, cherry-cheek little girl ran up out of breath, with a smile on her young, happy face, and without taking any notice of the gentleman, cried out with great joy, "Look here, father, only see how much I have got today!"

Mr. Johnson was much struck with her simplicity, but puzzled to know what was the occasion of this great joy. On

---

* 'potecary's—apothecary or pharmacy.
† 'natomy—anatomy or a skeleton.

looking at her, he perceived a small quantity of coarse wool, some of which had found its way through the holes of her clean, but scanty and ragged, woolen apron.

The father said, "This has been a successful day indeed, Molly; but don't you see the gentleman?"

Molly now made a low courtesy down to the very ground; while Mr. Johnson inquired into the cause of the mutual satisfaction which both father and daughter had expressed at the unusual good fortune of the day.

"Sir," said the shepherd, "poverty is a great sharpener of the wits. My wife and I cannot endure to see our children, poor as they are, without shoes and stockings, not only on account of the pinching cold, which cramps their poor little limbs, but because it degrades and debases them; and poor people who have but little regard to appearance, will seldom be found to have any great regard to honesty and goodness. I don't say this is always the case, but I am sure it is so too often. Now, shoes and stockings being very dear, we never could afford to get them without a little contrivance. I must show you how I manage about the shoes, when you condescend to call at our cottage, sir; as to stockings, this is one way we take to help to get them.

"My young ones, who are too little to do much work, sometimes wander at odd hours over the hills for the chance of finding what little wool the sheep may drop when they rub themselves, as they are apt to do, against the bushes.* These scattered bits of wool the children pick up out of the brambles, which I see have torn sad holes in Molly's apron today; they carry this wool home, and when

* This piece of frugal industry is a real fact; as is the character of the shepherd, and his uncommon knowledge of the Scriptures.

they have got a pretty parcel together, their mother cards
it; for she can sit and card in the chimney corner, when she
is not able to wash or work about the house. The biggest
girl then spins it. It does very well for us without dyeing,
for poor people must not stand for the color of their stockings. After this, our little boys knit it for themselves, while
they are employed in crow-keeping in the fields, and after
they get home at night. As for the knitting which the girls
and their mother do, that is chiefly for sale, which helps to
pay our rent."

Mr. Johnson lifted up his eyes in silent astonishment at
the shifts which honest poverty can make, rather than beg
or steal; and was surprised to think how many ways of
subsisting there are, which those who live at their ease
little suspect. He secretly resolved to be more attentive to
his own petty expenses than he had hitherto been; and to
be more watchful that nothing was wasted in his family.

But to return to the shepherd. Mr. Johnson told him
that as he must needs be at his friend's house, who lived
many miles off, that night, he could not, as he wished to
do, make a visit to his cottage at present. "But I will certainly do it," said he, "on my return, for I long to see your
wife and her nice little family, and to be an eyewitness of
her neatness and good management."

The poor man's tears started into his eyes on hearing
the commendations bestowed on his wife; and wiping them
off with the sleeve of his coat, for he was not worth a
handkerchief in the world, he said, "O, sir, you just now, I
am afraid, called me a humble man, but indeed I am a very
proud one."

"Proud!" exclaimed Mr. Johnson, "I hope not; pride is a

great sin, and as the poor are liable to it as well as the rich, so good a man as you seem to be ought to guard against it."

"Sir," said he, "you are right, but I am not proud of myself; God knows I have nothing to be proud of. I am a poor sinner; but indeed, sir, I am proud of my wife; she is not only the most tidy, notable woman on the plain, but she is the kindest wife and mother, and the most contented, thankful Christian that I know. Last year I thought I should have lost her in a violent fit of the rheumatism, caught by going to work too soon after her lying-in,* I fear; for 'tis but a bleak, coldish place, as you may see, sir, in winter; and sometimes the snow lies so long under the hill, that I can hardly make myself a path to get out and buy a few necessaries in the next village; and we are afraid to send out the children, for fear they would be lost when the snow is deep.

"So, as I was saying, the poor soul was very bad indeed, and for several weeks, lost the use of all her limbs except her hands; a merciful Providence spared her the use of these, so that when she could not turn in her bed, she could contrive to patch a rag or two for her family. She was always saying, had it not been for the great goodness of God, she might have had her hands lame as well as her feet, or the palsy instead of the rheumatism, and then she could have done nothing—but nobody had so many mercies as she had.

"I will not tell you what we suffered during the bitter weather, sir; but my wife's faith and patience during that trying time, were as good a lesson to me as any sermon I

---

* Lying-in—the act of bearing a child.

could hear; and yet Mr. Jenkins gave us very comfortable ones too, that helped to keep up my spirits."

"I fear, shepherd," said Mr. Johnson, "you have found this to be but a bad world."

"Yes, sir," replied the shepherd, "but it is governed by a good God. And though my trials have now and then been sharp, why, then, sir, as the saying is, if the pain be violent, it is seldom lasting; and if be but moderate, why, then we can bear it the longer; and when it is quite taken away, ease is the more precious, and gratitude is quickened by the remembrance: thus, every way, and in every case, I can always find out a reason for vindicating Providence."

"But," said Mr. Johnson, "how do you do to support yourself under the pressure of actual want? Is not hunger a great weakener of your faith?"

"Sir," replied the shepherd, "I endeavor to live upon the promises. You, who abound in the good things of this world, are apt to set too high a value on them. Suppose, sir, the king, seeing me hard at work, were to say to me, that, if I would patiently work on till Christmas, a fine palace and a great estate should be the reward of my labors. Do you think, sir, that a little hunger, or a little cold, or a little wet, would make me flinch, when I was sure that a few months would put me in possession? Should I not say to myself, frequently, Cheer up, shepherd; 'tis but till Christmas? Now, is there not much less difference between this supposed day and Christmas, when I should take possession of the estate and palace, than there is between time and eternity, when I am sure of entering on a kingdom not made with hands? There is some comparison between a moment and a thousand years, because a thousand years

are made up of moments, all time being made up of the
same sort of stuff, as I may say; while there is no sort of
comparison between the longest portion of time and eternity. You know, sir, there is no way of measuring two things,
one of which has length and breadth, which shows it must
have an end somewhere; and another thing, being eternal,
is without end and without measure."

"But," said Mr. Johnson, "is not the fear of death sometimes to strong for your faith?"

"Blessed be God, sir," replied the shepherd, "the dark pas-
sage through the valley of the shadow of death is made safe
by the power of Him who conquered death. I know, indeed,
we shall go as naked out of this world as we came into it; but
an humble penitent will not be found naked in the other
world, sir. My Bible tells me of garments of praise and robes
of righteousness. And is it not a support, sir, under any of the
petty difficulties and distresses here, to be assured by the
word of him who cannot lie, that those who were in white
robes came out of the great tribulation? But, sir, I beg your
pardon for being so talkative. Indeed, you great folks can
hardly imagine how it raises and cheers a poor man's heart,
when such as you condescend to talk familiarly to him on
religious subjects. It seems to be a practical comment on the
text which says, 'The rich and the poor meet together: the
Lord is the Maker of them all.'* And so far from creating
disrespect, sir, and that nonsensical wicked notion about
equality, it rather prevents it. But to return to my wife.

"One Sunday afternoon when my wife was at the worst,
as I was coming out of church—for I went one part of the
day, and my eldest daughter the other, so my poor wife

---

* Proverbs 22:2—The rich and poor meet together: the LORD is the maker of them all.

was never left alone—as I was coming out of church, I say, Mr. Jenkins the minister called out to me, and asked me how my wife did, saying he had been kept from coming to see her by the deep fall of snow; and indeed from the parsonage-house to my hovel it was quite impassable. I gave him all the particulars he asked, and I am afraid a good many more, for my heart was quite full. He kindly gave me a shilling, and said he would certainly try to pick out his way, and come and see her in a day or two.

"While he was talking to me, a plain, farmer-looking gentleman in boots, who stood by, listened to all I said, but seemed to take no notice. It was Mr. Jenkins' wife's father, who was come to pass the Christmas-holidays at the parsonage-house. I had always heard him spoken of as a plain frugal man, who lived close himself, but was remarked to give away more than any of his show-away neighbors.

"Well, I went home with great spirits at this seasonable and unexpected supply; for we had tapped our last sixpence, and there was little work to be had on account of the weather. I told my wife I had not come back empty-handed. 'No, I dare say not,' says she, 'you have been serving a Master "who filleth the hungry with good things, though he sendeth the rich empty away."'*

"'True, Mary,' said I, 'we seldom fail to get good spiritual food from Mr. Jenkins, but today he has kindly supplied our bodily wants.'

"She was more thankful when I showed her the shilling, than I dare say some of your great people are when they get a hundred pounds."

Mr. Johnson's heart smote him when he heard such a

---

* Luke 1:53—He hath filled the hungry with good things; and the rich he hath sent empty away.

value set upon a shilling. "Surely," said he to himself, "I will never waste another;" but he said nothing to the shepherd, who thus pursued his story:—

"Next morning, before I went out, I sent a part of the money to buy a little ale and brown sugar, to put into her water-gruel; which you know, sir, made it nice and nourishing. I went out to cleave wood in a farm-yard, for there was no standing out on the plain, after such a snow as had fallen in the night. I went with a lighter heart than usual, because I had left my poor wife a little better, and comfortably supplied for this day, and I now resolved more than ever to trust God for the supplies of the next.

"When I came back at night, my wife fell a crying as soon as she saw me. This, I own, I thought but a bad return for the blessings she had so lately received, and so I told her.

"'O,' said she, 'it is too much, we are too rich; I am now frightened, not lest we should have no portion in this world, but for fear we should have our whole portion in it. Look here, John!'

"So saying she uncovered the bed whereon she lay, and showed me two warm, thick, new blankets. I could not believe my own eyes, sir, because when I went out in the morning I had left her with no other covering than our little, old, thin, blue rug. I was still more amazed when she put half a crown into my hand, telling me she had had a visit from Mr. Jenkins and Mr. Jones, the latter of whom had bestowed all these good things upon us. Thus, sir, have our lives been crowned with mercies. My wife got about again, and I do believe, under Providence, it was owing to these comforts; for the rheumatism, sir, without blankets by night and flannel by day, is but a baddish job, especially to people who have but little or no fire. She will always be a weakly body; but, thank God, her soul prospers and is in health. But I beg your pardon, sir, for talking on at this rate."

"Not at all, not at all," said Mr. Johnson; "I am much pleased with your story; you shall certainly see me in a few days. Goodnight." So saying, he slipped a crown into his hand and rode off.

"Surely," said the shepherd, "'goodness and mercy have followed me all the days of my life,'"[*] as he gave the money to his wife when he got home at night.

As to Mr. Johnson, he found abundant matter for his thoughts during the rest of his journey. On the whole he was more disposed to envy than to pity the shepherd. "I have seldom seen." said he, "so happy a man. It is a sort of happiness which the world could not give, and which, I plainly see, it has not been able to take away. This must be the true spirit of religion. I see more and more, that true goodness is not merely a thing of words and opinions, but a living principle brought into every common action of a man's life. What else could have supported this poor couple under every bitter trial of want and sickness? No, my honest shepherd, I do not pity, but I respect and even honor thee; and I will visit thy poor hovel on my return to Salisbury, with as much pleasure as I am now going to the house of my friend."

If Mr. Johnson keeps his word in sending me the account of his visit to the shepherd's cottage, I shall be very glad to entertain my readers with it.

---

[*] Psalm 23:6—Surely goodness and mercy shall follow me all the days of my life: and I will dwell in the house of the LORD for ever.

PART II

I AM willing to hope that my readers will not be sorry to hear some further particulars of their old acquaintance, the shepherd of Salisbury Plain. They will call to mind, that at the end of the first part, he was returning home, full of gratitude for the favors he had received from Mr. Johnson, whom we left pursuing his journey, after having promised to make a visit to the shepherd's cottage.

Mr. Johnson, after having passed some time with his friend, set out on his return to Salisbury, and on the Saturday evening reached a very small inn, a mile or two distant from the shepherd's village; for he never traveled on a Sunday. He went next morning to the church nearest the house where he passed the night; and after taking such refreshment as he could get at that house, he walked on to find out the shepherd's cottage.

His reason for visiting him on Sunday was chiefly because he supposed it to be the only day which the shepherd's employment allowed him to pass at home with his family; and as Mr. Johnson had been struck with his talk, he thought it would be neither unpleasant nor unprofitable to observe how a man who carried such an appearance of piety, spent his Sunday; for though he was so low in the world, this gentleman was not above entering very closely into his character, of which he thought he should be able to form a better judgment, by seeing whether his practice at home kept pace with his profession abroad. For it is not so much by observing how people talk, as how they live, that we ought to judge of their characters.

After a pleasant walk, Mr. Johnson got within sight of the cottage, to which he was directed by the clump of hawthorns and the broken chimney. He wished to take the family by surprise; and walking gently up to the house, he stood a while to listen. The door being half open, he saw the shepherd—who looked so respectable in his Sunday coat, that he should hardly have known him—his wife, and their numerous family drawing round their little table, which was covered with a clean, though very coarse cloth. There stood on it a large dish of potatoes, a brown pitcher, and a piece of coarse loaf. The wife and children stood in silent attention, while the shepherd, with uplifted hands and eyes, devoutly begged the blessing of heaven on their homely fare. Mr. Johnson could not help sighing to reflect, that he had sometimes seen better dinners eaten with less appearance of thankfulness.

The shepherd and his wife then sat down with great seeming cheerfulness, but the children stood; and while the mother was helping them, little fresh-colored Molly, who had picked the wool from the bushes with so much delight, cried out, "Father, I wish I was big enough to say grace; I am sure I should say it very heartily today, for I was thinking, what must *poor* people do, who have no salt to their potatoes; and do but look, our dish is quite full." "That is the true way of thinking, Molly," said the father; "in whatever concerns bodily wants and bodily comforts, it is our duty to compare our own lot with the lot of those who are worse off, and this will keep us thankful. On the other

THE SHEPHERD BEGGED THE BLESSING OF HEAVEN ON THEIR HOMELY FARE.

hand, whenever we are tempted to set up our own wisdom or goodness, we must compare ourselves with those who are wiser and better, and that will keep us humble."

Molly was now so hungry, and found the potatoes so good, that she had no time to make any more remarks; but was devouring her dinner very heartily, when the barking of the great dog drew her attention from her trencher* to the door, and spying the stranger, she cried out, "Look, father, see here; is not that the good gentleman?"

Mr. Johnson, finding himself discovered, immediately walked in, and was heartily welcomed by the honest shep- herd, who told his wife that this was the gentleman to whom they were so much obliged.

The good woman began, as some very neat people are rather too apt to do, with making many apologies, that her house was not cleaner, and that things were not in fitter order to receive such a gentleman. Mr. Johnson, however, on looking round, could discover nothing but the most perfect neatness. The trenchers on which they were eating were almost as white as their linen; and notwithstanding the number and smallness of the children, there was not the least appearance of dirt or litter.

The furniture was very simple and poor, hardly indeed amounting to bare necessaries. It consisted of four brown wooden chairs, which by constant rubbing, had become as bright as a looking-glass; an iron pot and kettle; a poor old grate, which scarcely held a handful of coal, and out of which the little fire that had been in it appeared to have been taken as soon as it had answered the end for which it had been lighted, that of boiling their potatoes. Over the

---

* Trencher—a wooden platter used to serve food.

chimney stood an old-fashioned broad bright candlestick, and a still brighter spit; it was pretty clear that this last was kept rather for ornament than use.

An old carved elbow-chair, and a chest of the same date which stood in the corner, were considered as the most valuable part of the shepherd's goods, having been in his family for three generations.

But all these were lightly esteemed by him, in comparison of another possession, which, added to the above, made up the whole of what he had inherited from his father; and which last he would not have parted with, if no other could have been had, for a king's ransom: this was a large old Bible, which lay on the window-seat, neatly covered with brown cloth, variously patched. This sacred book was most reverently preserved from dog's-ears, dirt, and every other injury, but such as time and much use had made it suffer in spite of care. On the clean white walls were pasted a hymn on the crucifixion of our Savior, a print of the Prodigal Son, the Shepherd's Hymn,* a "New History of a True Book,"† and "Patient Joe, or the Newcastle Collier."‡

After the first salutations were over, Mr. Johnson said that if they would go on quietly with their dinner, he would sit down. Though a good deal ashamed, they thought it more respectful to obey the gentleman, who, having cast his eye on their slender provisions, gently rebuked the shepherd for not having indulged himself, as it was Sunday, with a morsel of bacon to relish his potatoes.

The shepherd said nothing, but poor Mary colored and hung down her head, saying, "Indeed, sir, it is not my

---

* The Shepherd's Hymn or "The Lord My Pasture Shall Prepare," by Joseph Addison. (Page 82.)
† "A New History of a True Book"—a Cheap Repository Tract.
‡ "Patient Joe, or the Newcastle Collier"—a poem by Hannah More.

fault; I did beg my husband to allow himself a bit of meat today out of your honor's bounty; but he was too good to do it, and it is all for my sake."

The shepherd seemed unwilling to come to an explanation, but Mr. Johnson desired Mary to go on. So she continued, "You must know, sir, that both of us, next to a sin, dread a debt, and indeed in some cases a debt is a sin; but with all our care and pains we have never been able quite to pay off the doctor's bill for that bad fit of rheumatism which I had last winter. Now, when you were pleased to give my husband that kind present the other day, I heartily desired him to buy a bit of meat for Sunday, as I said before, that he might have a little refreshment out of your kindness. 'But,' he answered, 'Mary, it is never out of my mind long together, that we still owe a few shillings to the doctor,' and thank God, it was all we did owe in the world. 'Now, if I carry him this money directly, it will not only show him our honesty and our good will, but it will be an encouragement to him to come to you another time, in case you should be taken once more in such a bad fit; for I must own,' added my poor husband, 'that the thought of your being so terribly ill, without any help, is the only misfortune that I want courage to face.'"

Here the grateful woman's tears ran down so fast that she could not go on. She wiped them with the corner of her apron, and humbly begged pardon for making so free.

"Indeed, sir," said the shepherd, "though my wife is full as unwilling to be in debt as myself, yet I could hardly prevail on her to consent to my paying this money just then, because she said it was hard I should not have a taste of the gentleman's bounty myself. But for once, sir, I would have my own way. For you must know, as I pass the best part of my time alone, tending my sheep, 'tis a great point with me, sir, to get comfortable matter for my own thoughts; so that 'tis rather self-interest in me, to allow myself no pleasures and no practices that wont bear thinking on over and over. For when one is a good deal alone, you know, sir, all one's bad deeds do so rush in upon one, as I may say, and so torment one, that there is no true comfort to be had, but in keeping clear of wrong doings and false pleasures; and that I suppose may be one reason why so many folks hate to stay a bit by themselves.

"But, as I was saying, when I came to think the matter over on the hill yonder, said I to myself, a good dinner is a good thing, I grant, and yet it will be but cold comfort to me a week after, to be able to say—to be sure I had a nice shoulder of mutton last Sunday for dinner, thanks to the good gentleman, but then I am in debt—I *had* a rare dinner, that's certain; but the pleasure of that has long been over, and the debt still remains—I have spent the crown, and now if my poor wife should be taken in one of those fits again, die she must, unless God work a miracle to prevent it, for I can get no help for her. This thought settled all; and I set off directly and paid the crown to the doctor with as much cheerfulness as I could have felt on sitting down to the fattest shoulder of mutton that was ever roasted. And if I was contented at the time, think how much more happy I have been at the remembrance! O sir, there are no pleasures worth the name, but such as bring no plague or penitence after them."

Mr. Johnson was satisfied with the shepherd's reasons, and agreed, that though a good dinner was not to be despised, yet it was not worthy to be compared with a "contented mind," which, as the proverb truly says, "is a continual feast."*

"But come," said the good gentleman, "what have we got in this brown mug?"

"As good water," said the shepherd, "as any in the king's dominions. I have heard of countries beyond sea, in which there is no wholesome water; nay, I have been myself in a great town not far off; where they are obliged to buy all the water they get, while a good Providence sends to my very door a spring as clear and fine as Jacob's well. When I am tempted to repine that I have often no other drink, I call to mind that it was nothing better than a cup of cold water which the woman of Samaria drew for the greatest guest that ever visited this world."

"Very well," replied Mr. Johnson; "but as your honesty has made you prefer a poor meal to being in debt, I will at least send and get something for you to drink. I saw a little public-house† just by the church, as I came along. Let that little rosy-faced fellow fetch a mug of beer."

So saying, he looked full at the boy, who did not offer to stir; but cast an eye at his father, to know what he was to do.

"Sir," said the shepherd, "I hope we shall not appear un-grateful, if we seem to refuse your favor; my little boy would, I am sure, fly to serve you on any other occasion. But, good sir, it is Sunday, and should any of my family be seen at a public-house on a Sabbath-day, it would be a much greater grief to me than to drink water all my life. I am often talking against these doings to others; and if I

---

* Proverbs 15:15—All the days of the afflicted are evil: but he that is of a merry heart hath a continual feast.
† Public-house—a pub or drinking establishment.

should say one thing and do another, you can't think what an advantage it would give many of my neighbors over me, who would be glad enough to report, that they caught the shepherd's son at the alehouse, without explaining how it happened. Christians, you know, sir, must be doubly watchful, or they will not only bring disgrace on them-selves, but what is much worse, on that holy name by which they are called."

"Are you not a little too cautious, my honest friend?" said Mr. Johnson.

"I humbly ask your pardon, sir," replied the shepherd, "if I think that is impossible. In my poor notion, I no more understand how a man can be too cautious, than how he can be too strong, or too healthy."

"You are right, indeed," said Mr. Johnson, "as a general principle; but this struck me as a very small thing."

"Sir," said the shepherd, "I am afraid you will think me very bold, but you encourage me to speak out."

"'Tis what I wish," said the gentleman.

"Then, sir," resumed the shepherd, "I doubt if, where there is a temptation to do wrong, any thing can be called small; that is, in short, if there is any such thing as a small willful sin. A poor man, like me, is seldom called out to do great things, so that it is not by a few striking deeds his character can be judged by his neighbors, but by the little round of daily customs he allows himself in."

"I should like," said Mr. Johnson, "to know how you manage, in this respect."

"I am but a poor scholar, sir," replied the shepherd, "but I have made myself a little sort of rule. I always avoid, as I am an ignorant man, picking out any one single difficult text to distress my mind about, or to go and build opinions upon, because I know that puzzles and injures poor un‑learned Christians. But I endeavor to collect what is the *general* spirit or meaning of Scripture on any particular subject, by putting a few texts together, which though I find them dispersed up and down, yet all seem to look the same way, to prove the same truth, or hold out the same comfort. So, when I am tried or tempted, or any thing happens in which I am at a loss what to do, I apply to my rule—to the 'law and the testimony.' To be sure, I can't always find a particular direction, as to the very case, because then the Bible must have been bigger than all those great books I once saw in the library at Salisbury Palace, which the butler told me were acts of parliament; and, had that been the case, a poor man would never have had money to buy, nor a working man time to read, the Bible; and so Christianity could only have been a religion for the rich, for those who had money and leisure; which, blessed be God! is so far from being the truth, that in all that fine discourse of our Savior to John's disciples, it is enough to reconcile any poor man in the world to his low condition, to observe, when Christ reckons up the things for which he came on earth; to observe, I say, what he keeps for last: 'Go, tell John,' says he, 'those things which ye do hear and see; the blind receive their sight, and the lame walk, the lepers are cleansed, and the deaf hear, and the dead are raised up.'* Now, sir, all these are wonders, to be sure, but they are nothing to what follows. They are but like the lower rounds of a ladder, as I may say, by which

---

* Matthew 11:4,5—Jesus answered and said unto them, Go and shew John again those things which ye do hear and see: The blind receive their sight, and the lame walk, the lepers are cleansed, and the deaf hear, the dead are raised up, and the poor have the gospel preached to them.

you mount to the top—'and the poor have the Gospel preached to them.' I dare say, if John had had any doubts before, this last part of the message must have cleared them up at once. For it must have made him certain sure at once, that a religion which placed preaching salvation to the poor above healing the sick, which ranked the soul above the body, and set heaven above health, must have come from God,"

"But," said Mr. Johnson, "you say you can generally pick out your particular duty from the Bible, though that immediate duty be not fully explained."

"Indeed, sir," replied the shepherd, "I think I can find out the principle, at least, if I bring but a willing mind. The want of that is the great hindrance. 'Whoso doeth my will, he shall know of the doctrine.'* You know that text, sir. I believe a stubborn will makes the Bible harder to be understood than any want of learning. 'Tis corrupt affections which blind the understanding, sir. The more a man hates sin, the clearer he will see his way; and the more he loves holiness, the better he will understand his Bible. The more practical conviction will he get of that pleasant truth, that 'the secret of the Lord is with them that fear him.'† Now, sir, suppose I had time and learning, and possessed all the books I saw at the bishop's, where could I find out a surer way to lay the axe to the root of all covetousness, selfishness, and injustice, than the plain and ready rule, 'to do unto all men as I would they should do unto me?'‡ If my neighbor does me an injury, can I be at any loss how to

---

* John 7:17—If any man will do his will, he shall know of the doctrine, whether it be of God, or whether I speak of myself.
† Psalm 25:14—The secret of the LORD is with them that fear him; and he will shew them his covenant.
‡ Matthew 7:12—So in everything, do to others what you would have them do to you, for this sums up the Law and the Prophets.

proceed with him, when I recollect the parable of the unforgiving steward, who refused to pardon a debt of an hundred pence, when his own ten thousand talents had been remitted to him? I defy any man to retain habitual selfishness, hardness of heart, or any other allowed sin, who daily and conscientiously tries his own heart by this touchstone. The straight rule will show the crooked prac‐ tice to every one who honestly tries the one by the other."

"Why, you seem to make Scripture a thing of general application," said Mr. Johnson, "in cases to which many, I fear, do not apply it."

"It applies to every thing, sir," replied the shepherd. "When those men who are now disturbing the peace of the world, and trying to destroy the confidence of God's chil‐ dren in their Maker and their Savior; when those men, I say, came to my poor hovel with their new doctrines and their new books, I would never look into one of them: for I remembered it was the first sin of the first pair to lose their innocence for the sake of a little wicked knowledge; besides, my own Book told me 'to fear God and honor the king—to meddle not with them who are given to change— not to speak evil of dignities—to render honor to whom honor is due.' So that I was furnished with a little coat of mail,* as I may say, which preserved me, while those who had no such armor fell into the snare."

While they were thus talking, the children, who had stood very quietly behind, and had not stirred a foot, now began to scamper about all at once, and in a moment ran to the window-seat to pick up their little old hats. Mr. Johnson looked surprised at this disturbance; the shepherd

---

* Mail—flexible armor made of interlinked rings.

asked his pardon, telling him it was the sound of the church bell which had been the cause of their rudeness; for their mother had brought them up with such a fear of being too late for church, that it was but who could catch the first stroke of the bell, and be first ready. He had always taught them to think that nothing was more indecent than to get into church after it was begun; for as the service opened with an exhortation to repentance; and a confession of sin, it looked very presumptuous not to be ready to join in it; it looked as if people did not feel themselves to be sinners. And though such as lived at a great distance might plead difference of clocks as an excuse, yet those who lived within the sound of the bell could pretend neither ignorance nor mistake.

Mary and her children set forward. Mr. Johnson and the shepherd followed, taking care to talk the whole way on such subjects as might fit them for the solemn duties of the place to which they were going.

"I have often been sorry to observe," said Mr. Johnson, "that many, who are reckoned decent, good kind of people, and who would on no account neglect going to church, yet seem to care but little in what frame or temper of mind they go thither. They will talk of their worldly concerns till they get within the door, and then take them up again the very minute the sermon is over, which makes me ready to fear they lay too much stress on the mere form of going to a place of worship. Now, for my part, I always find that it requires a little time to bring my mind into a state fit to do any *common* business well, much more this great and most necessary business of all."

"Yes, sir," said the shepherd, "and then I think, too, how

busy I should be in preparing my mind, if I was going into the presence of a great gentleman, or a lord, or a king; and shall the King of kings be treated with less respect? Besides, one likes to see people feel as if going to church was a thing of choice and pleasure, as well as a duty, and that they were as desirous not to be the last there, as they would be if they were going to a feast or a fair."

After service, Mr. Jenkins the clergyman, who was well acquainted with the character of Mr. Johnson, and had a great respect for him, accosted him with much civility; expressing his concern that he could not enjoy just now so much of his conversation as he wished, as he was obliged to visit a sick person at a distance, but hoped to have a little talk with him before he left the village. As they walked along together, Mr. Johnson made such inquiries about the shepherd as served to confirm him in the high opinion he entertained of his piety, good sense, industry, and self-denial. They parted, the clergyman promising to call in at the cottage on his way home.

The shepherd, who took it for granted that Mr. Johnson was gone to the parsonage, walked home with his wife and children, and was beginning in his usual way to catechize and instruct his family, when Mr. Johnson came in, and insisted that the shepherd should go on with his instructions just as if he were not there. This gentleman, who was very desirous of being useful to his own servants and workmen in the way of religious instruction, was sometimes sorry to find, that though he took a good deal of pains, they did not now and then quite understand him; for though his meaning was very good, his language was not always very plain; and though the *things* he said were not hard to be understood, yet the *words* were, especially to such as were very ignorant. And he now began to find out, that if people were ever so wise and good, yet if they had not a simple, agreeable, and familiar way of expressing themselves, some of their plain hearers would not be much the better for them. For this reason he was not above listening to the plain, humble way, in which this honest man taught his family: for though he knew that he himself had many advantages over the shepherd, had more learning, and could teach him many things; yet he was not too proud to learn, even of so poor a man, in any point where he thought the shepherd might have the advantage of him.

This gentleman was much pleased with the knowledge and piety he discovered in the answers of the children; and desired the shepherd to tell him how he contrived to keep up a sense of divine things in his own mind, and in that of his family, with so little leisure and so little reading.

"O, as to that, sir," said the shepherd, "we do not read much except in one book, to be sure, but with my hearty prayer for God's blessing on the use of that book, what little knowledge is needful seems to come of course, as it were. And my chief study has been, to bring the fruits of the Sunday reading into the week's business, and to keep up the same sense of God in the heart, when the Bible is in the cupboard, as when it is in the hand. In short, to apply what I read in the book to what I meet with in the field."

"I don't quite understand you," said Mr. Johnson.

"Sir," replied the shepherd, "I have but a poor gift at conveying these things to others, though I have much comfort from them in my own mind; but I am sure that the most ignorant and hard-working people, who are in earnest about their salvation, may help to keep up devout thoughts and good affections during the week, though they have hardly any time to look at a book. And it will help them to keep out bad thoughts, too, which is no small matter. But then they must know the Bible; they must have read the word of God diligently; that is a kind of stock in trade for a Christian to set up with; and it is this which makes me so diligent in teaching it to my children, and even in storing their memories with psalms and chapters. This is a great help to a poor, hard-working man, who will scarcely meet with any thing but what he may turn to some good account. If one lives in the fear and love of God, almost every thing one sees abroad will teach one to adore his power and goodness, and bring to mind some text of Scripture, which shall fill the heart with thankfulness and the mouth with praise. When I look upwards, 'the heavens declare the glory of God;'* and shall I be silent and ungrateful? If I look round and see the valleys standing thick with corn, how can I help blessing that Power who 'giveth me all things richly to enjoy?'† I may learn gratitude from the beasts of the field, for the 'ox knoweth his owner, and the ass his master's crib;'‡ and shall a Christian not know, shall a Christian not consider what great things God has done for him? I, who am a shepherd, endeavor to fill my soul with a constant remembrance of that good Shepherd, who 'feedeth me in green pastures, and maketh me to lie down beside the still waters,' and

---

* Psalm 19:1—The heavens declare the glory of God; and the firmament sheweth his handywork.
† 1 Timothy 6:17—Charge them that are rich in this world, that they be not highminded, nor trust in uncertain riches, but in the living God, who giveth us richly all things to enjoy.
‡ Isaiah 1:3—The ox knoweth his owner, and the ass his master's crib: but Israel doth not know, my people doth not consider.

'whose rod and staff comfort me.'* A religion, sir, which has its seat in the heart, and its fruits in the life, takes up little time in the study. And yet, in another sense, true religion, which from sound principal brings forth right practice, fills up the whole time, and life too, as one may say."

"You are happy," said Mr. Johnson, "in this retired life, by which you escape the corruptions of the world."

"Sir," said the shepherd, "I do not escape the corruptions of my own evil nature. Even there, on that wild solitary hill, I can find out that my heart is prone to evil thoughts. I suppose, sir, that different states have different temptations. You great folks that live in the world, perhaps are exposed to some, of which such a poor man as I am knows nothing. But to one who leads a lonely life like me, evil thoughts are a chief besetting sin; and I can no more withstand these without the grace of God, than a rich gentleman can withstand the snares of evil company, without the same grace. And I feel that I stand in need of God's help continually, and if he should give me up to my own evil heart, I should be lost."

Mr. Johnson approved of the shepherd's sincerity, for he had always observed, that where there was no humility, and no watchfulness against sin, there was no religion; and he said, that the man who did not feel himself to be a sinner, in his opinion could not be a Christian.

Just as they were in this part of their discourse, Mr. Jenkins the clergyman came in. After the usual

---

* Psalm 23:2-4—He maketh me to lie down in green pastures: he leadeth me beside the still waters. He restoreth my soul: he leadeth me in the paths of righteousness for his name's sake. Yea, though I walk through the valley of the shadow of death, I will fear no evil: for thou art with me; thy rod and thy staff they comfort me.

salutations, he said, "Well, shepherd, I wish you joy: I know you will be sorry to gain any advantage by the death of a neighbor; but old Wilson, my clerk, was so infirm, and I trust so well prepared, that there is no reason to be sorry for his death. I have been to pray with him, but he died while I staid. I have always intended you should succeed to his place; 'tis no great matter of profit, but every little is something."

"No great matter, sir!" cried the shepherd; "indeed it is a great matter to me; it will more than pay my rent. Blessed be God for all his goodness." Mary said nothing, but lifted up her eyes, full of tears, in silent gratitude.

"I am glad of this little circumstance," said Mr. Jenkins, "not only for your sake, but for the sake of the office itself. I so heartily reverence every religious institution, that I would never have even the *Amen* added to the excellent prayers of our church by vain or profane lips; and, if it depended on me, there should be no such thing in the land as an idle, drunken, or irreligious parish-clerk. Sorry I am to say, that this matter is not always sufficiently attended to, and that I know some of a very indifferent character."

Mr. Johnson now inquired of the clergyman whether there were many children in the parish.

"More than you would expect," replied he, "from the seeming smallness of it, but there are some little hamlets which you do not see."

"I think," returned Mr. Johnson, "I recollect that in the conversation I had with the shepherd on the hill yonder, he told me you had no Sunday school."

"I am sorry to say we have none," said the minister; "I do what I can to remedy this misfortune by public catechizing; but having two or three churches to serve, I cannot give so much time as I wish to private instruction; and having a large family of my own, and no assistance from others, I have never been able to establish a school."

"There is an excellent institution in London," said Mr. Johnson, "called the Sunday School Society, which kindly gives books and other helps, on the application of such pious ministers as stand in need of their aid, and which I am sure, would have assisted you; but I think we shall be able to do something ourselves. Shepherd," continued he, "if I were a king, and had it in my power to make you a rich and a great man, with a word speaking, I would not do it. Those who are raised by some sudden stroke, much above the station in which divine Providence had placed them, seldom turn out good or very happy. I have never had any great things in my power, but as far as I have been able, I have always been glad to assist the worthy. I have, however, never attempted or desired to set any poor man much above his natural condition; but it is a pleasure to me to lend him such assistance as may make that condition more easy to himself; and to put him in a way which shall call him to the performance of more duties than perhaps he could have performed without my help, and of performing them in a better manner. What rent do you pay for this cottage?"

"Fifty shillings a year, sir."

"It is in a sad, tattered condition; is there not a better to be had in the village?"

"That in which the poor clerk lived," said the clergyman, "is not only more tight and whole, but has two decent chambers, and a very large, light kitchen."

"That will be very convenient," replied Mr. Johnson;

"pray what is the rent?"

"I think," said the shepherd, "poor neighbor Wilson gave somewhere about four pounds a year, or it might be guineas."

"Very well," said Mr. Johnson, "and what will the clerk's place be worth, think you?"

"About three pounds," was the answer.

"Now," continued Mr. Johnson, "my plan is, that the shepherd should take that house immediately; for as the poor man is dead, there will be no need of waiting till quarter-day, if I make up the difference."

"True, sir," said Mr. Jenkins, "and I am sure my wife's father, whom I expect tomorrow, will willingly assist a little towards buying some of the clerk's old goods. And the sooner they remove the better, for poor Mary caught that bad rheumatism by sleeping under a leaky thatch."

The shepherd was too much moved to speak, and Mary could hardly sob out, "O, sir, you are too good; indeed, this house will do very well."

"It may do very well for you and your poor children, Mary," said Mr. Johnson gravely, "but it will not do for a school; the kitchen is neither large nor light enough. Shepherd," continued he, "with your good minister's leave and kind assistance, I propose to set up in this parish a Sunday-school, and to make you the master. It will not interfere with your weekly calling, and it is the only lawful way in which you can turn the Sabbath into a day of some little profit to your family, by doing, as I hope, a great deal of good to the souls of others. The rest of the week you will work as usual. The difference of rent between this house and the clerk's, I shall pay myself; for to put you in a better house at your own expense, would be no great kindness.

"As for honest Mary, who is not fit for hard labor, or any out-of-door work, I propose to endow a small weekly school, of which she shall be the mistress, and employ her notable turn to good account, by teaching ten or a dozen girls to knit, sew, spin, card, or any other useful way of getting their bread; for all this I shall only pay her the usual price, for I am not going to make you rich, but useful."

"Not rich, sir!" cried the shepherd. "How can I ever be thankful enough for such blessings? And will my poor Mary have a dry thatch overhead? And shall I be able to send for the doctor, when I am like to lose her? Indeed, my cup runs over with blessings. I hope God will give me humility."

Here he and Mary looked at each other and burst into tears. The gentlemen saw their distress, and kindly walked out upon the green before the door, that these honest people might give vent to their feelings.

As soon as they were alone they crept into one corner of the room, where they thought they could not be seen, and fell on their knees, devoutly blessing and praising God for his mercies. Never were heartier prayers presented than this grateful couple offered up for their benefactors. The warmth of their gratitude could only be equaled by the earnestness with which they besought the blessing of God on the work in which they were going to engage.

The two gentlemen now left this happy family, and walked to the parsonage, where the evening was spent in a manner very edifying to Mr. Johnson, who the next day took all proper measures for putting the shepherd in immediate possession of his now comfortable habitation. Mr. Jenkins' father-in-law, the worthy gentleman who gave the shepherd's wife the blankets, in the first part of this history, arrived at the parsonage before Mr. Johnson left it, and assisted in fitting up the clerk's cottage.

Mr. Johnson took his leave, promising to call on the worthy minister and his new clerk once a year, in his summer's journey over the plain, as long as it would please God to spare his life. He had every reason to be satisfied with the objects of his bounty. The shepherd's zeal and piety made him a blessing to the rising generation. The old resorted to his school for the benefit of hearing the young instructed; and the clergyman had the pleasure of seeing that he was rewarded, for the protection he gave the school, by the great increase in his congregation. The shepherd not only exhorted both parents and children to the indispensable duty of a regular attendance at church, but, by his pious counsels, he drew them thither, and, by his plain and prudent instructions, enabled them to understand, and of course delight in, the public worship of God.

THE SHEPHERD'S HYMN

The Lord my pasture shall prepare,
And feed me with a shepherd's care;
His presence shall my wants supply,
And guard me with a watchful eye:
My noon-day walks he shall attend,
And all my midnight hours defend.

When on the sultry glebe I faint,
Or on the thirsty mountain pant,
To fertile vales and dewy meads
My weary, wand'ring steps he leads,
Where peaceful rivers, soft and slow,
Amid the verdant landscape flow.

Though in the paths of death I tread,
With gloomy horrors overspread,
My steadfast heart shall fear no ill,
For thou, O Lord, art with me still;
Thy friendly arm shall give me aid,
And guide me through the dreadful shade.

Though in a bare and rugged way,
Through devious, lonely wilds I stray,
Thy bounty shall my pains beguile;
The barren wilderness shall smile,
With sudden greens and herbage crowned,
And streams shall murmur all around.

—Joseph Addison

A SHORT MEMOIR
OF
THE LATE DAVID SAUNDERS,
THE SHEPHERD OF SALISBURY PLAIN

FROM "THE EVANGELICAL MAGAZINE," 1805

TRUE Religion, is like the cut diamond, which reflects a luster in whatever position it may be placed. Religion gives dignity to the meanest condition of life, and confers happiness without the aid of riches. A striking proof of this occurs in the instance of David Saunders, of West Lavington, Wilts, better known to the world as "The Shepherd of Salisbury Plain;" being the undoubted subject of the beautiful tract, which, some years since, issued from the ingenious pen of Miss Hannah More, under that title.

David Saunders was born about the year 1717; and, in his youth, enjoyed the then distinguished privilege, among the lower class, of being taught to read, and particularly to read his Bible: and here we may observe the mistake of those persons who are afraid to teach children to read in the Scriptures, lest it should give them a dislike to them in after-life. It is easy, from other principles, to account for this distaste; the carnal mind has no natural relish for divine truth; and when men become vicious in their conduct, they very naturally become inimical to the Bible, because it will not tolerate their sins. There are innumerable instances, however, of the advantages of an early acquaintance with the sacred volume. How often has an awful text, riveted on the mind of youth, checked the career of Vice!—or a pertinent circumstance of Scripture-History guarded the mind from temptation, or supported the sinking spirits above despair! And when, in afterlife, it has pleased God to renew the heart, in circumstances unfavorable to reading. O what a treasure has the Christian found already stored in his memory, though hitherto but seldom recollected; for the traces of our first reading are generally the easiest to be recovered, and the last to be forgotten.

In early life, David was greatly afflicted with the leprosy; which, mentioning one day to a pious young man who was walking with him, he told him he had a much worse leprosy in his soul than in his body; and affectionately recommended him to the good Physician. He was prevailed on to go to hear a person preach in one of his master's fields; where he found out both his soul's disease and remedy. It may deserve mention as an awful circumstance, that a gentleman's servant, who violently opposed this minister, was soon after seized with the frenzy-fever, and died insane. We should not be hasty in pronouncing such cases instances of divine judgment, but we have often occasion to remark, that the same word which is made the savor of life to one person, is the savor of death unto another, through their rejection of its blessings.

While our young shepherd lived at Imber, which was before he married, after he had done work in the evening, he used to walk about eight miles to meet the people of God at Sceend; and return again the same night to be ready for his business early in the morning:—an admirable example of prudence, industry, and zeal united.—More than thirty years was he employed as the shepherd upon one farm. A long life of rural occupation must afford many materials for reflection; and his particular employment gave him much leisure for it. Besides, David conversed daily with his Bible, and always found matter there for his meditation; while every object in the field, the sheep, the pasture, the surrounding horizon, and his own occupation, had all a tendency to bring to his recollection a psalm, a prophecy, a parable, or some other blessed portion of the Scriptures.

Notwithstanding his humble situation and scanty means for supporting a family, David Saunders married. He did not reason as many do, who seem, to consider the increase of wealth as a grand object in entering upon this state: he considered the lilies of the field, how they grew; and he saw how the birds of the air were fed. God blessed him with a most excellent wife and a numerous offspring: he had sixteen children born, all baptized at the parish church; and twelve of them at one time, were "like olive-branches round about his table." It is not to be supposed that a poor shepherd, with such a family, could be without his difficulties, especially as his wife suffered much from sickness: but she was a most pious, notable woman; and all the children were brought up in early habits of industry. When trouble used to prey upon her spirits, her constant method was to repair, with cries and tears to her husband's large Bible, which he used to keep in the thatch of his cottage; and there, as her daughter has since informed the writer, she always found something to comfort or support her.

Her husband, good man, fled to the same resource in all his trials: his salary being but 6s. 3d. weekly, out of which he was sometimes obliged to pay a boy for assistance; but when times of peculiar necessity occurred, God always raised him up a friend. Dr. Stonehouse (afterwards Sir James) repeatedly assisted him; and sometimes his good neighbours, in humbler life, united to supply his wants. In one of his letters, in his old age, he thus writes, with much Christian simplicity: "As for my part, I am but very poorly in body, having very sore legs; and cannot perform the business of my flock without help. As to the things of this world, I have but little share,—having my little cot to pray and praise my God in, and a bed to rest on: so I have just as much of this world as I desire. But my garment is worn out; and some of my Christian friends think they must put their mites together and buy me one, or else I shall not be able to endure the cold in the winter: so I can say, Good is the Lord!—he is still fulfilling his promise, 'I will never leave thee, nor forsake thee!'"

At one time, having been obliged to apply to the parish officer for assistance, he was cruelly repulsed, under the pretence that he was a preacher, and got money by his preaching. David was compelled to summon the officer before a magistrate, where he made the same plea; but the good man denied the charge. He acknowledged, indeed, that, on a Sabbath-morning, before he went out to attend his sheep, he used to read his Bible, and sing and pray in his family; and if any of his neighbours came in to unite with him, as some-times many of them did, they were very welcome; and he did not know that he offended any law. The worthy magistrate, struck with the good man's simplicity, reproved the unfeeling overseer; telling him, he had better employ himself as well; and ordered him to give all the relief desired.

Good David Saunders was remarkably spiritual in his conversation; and though worldly business sometimes necessarily engrossed his attention, when that was done, he would say, "Now let us have something profitable;" or he would ask his Christian friends, "Is it agreeable to spend a little time in prayer?" When Mr. Stedman went to the neighbouring village of Cheverill, to settle as curate there to Dr. Stonehouse, the first person he met in that parish was our shepherd, who told him, in a conversation he had with him some time afterwards, that, taking the stranger to be the minister expected there, he could not help repeating to himself these words of St. Paul, "How beautiful are the feet of them that preach the gospel of peace, and bring glad tidings of good things!" The same clergyman adds, that he "had acquired a surprising knowledge of the Scriptures, readiness in prayer, and spiritual conversation." By "reading" his Bible "and prayer, he seemed to keep up a constant communion with God."

This good man was a happy instance of the attractive power of true religion: wherever he went, he was admired and beloved; even when he visited distant parts with his master's sheep for their wintering, the good people all around used to caress him, and delight to hear his pious and simple conversation; and when, about a year before his death; the loss of sight totally incapacitated him for his pastoral office (as it may be called) the neighbouring farmers invited him to visit them for a month together. It had been his constant prayer that the Lord would not let him long struggle with death, or lie long ill, to be trouble- some to his friends; and the Lord granted his request.

Being on a visit to one of his friends at Wyke, the dear

aged saint united, as usual, with the family in prayer; and was afterwards heard to pray with extraordinary fervency in his own room: he slept with the son of his kind host; and after he was in bed, began to open to him the things of God, and talked to him of the blessed Jesus till he fell asleep,—to wake no more till the resurrection of the just; for in the morning he was found dead! At the joint expense of his friends, and as a mark of their particular respect, his remains were conveyed to his own parish, where they were interred with more than usual solemnity, about the middle of September, 1796, and in the eightieth year of his age. Thus was he, as a shock of corn fully ripe, gathered into the garner of the Lord!

Miss More's admirable tract, before referred to, contains a just delineation of this extraordinary person; and tho' for many of the incidents we are, doubtless, indebted to her elegant and inventive pen, the reader will peruse it with new interest, when he finds the outlines to be faithful, and the conversations recited in perfect harmony with the real character of the man; for though "simple and unlearned," as the world would call him, he possessed uncommon natural abilities; and, what is far better, was endued with a large portion of that "wisdom which is from above,—pure and peaceable!"

INTRODUCTION TO
THE SHEPHERD'S LETTER

FROM "THE EVANGELICAL MAGAZINE," 1803

To the Editor.

Sir,

Many of your readers, without doubt, have read, with pleasure and instruction, the little cheap Repository Tract, entitled, "The Shepherd of Salisbury Plain." Some, per-haps, may not know that the admirable account was founded on a real character and facts. Having met with an Original Letter, in the Shepherd's own hand-writing, ad-dressed to a respectable Farmer, I have thought it may be acceptable to your readers to insert it in your Magazine, with no other alterations than in the spelling of a few words, and the omission of a few repetitions and a para-graph or two.—A short account of his death, from a London Newspaper, of September 15, 1796, may properly be in-serted, as a sort of Preface to the Letter.

I am yours, & etc.

Basingstoke.

JOSEPH JEFFERSON.

OBITUARY OF DAVID SAUNDERS

FROM A LONDON NEWSPAPER, SEPTEMBER 15th, 1796

"Last week died, at Wyke, between Bath and Bristol, in the seventieth year of his age, David Saunders, of West Lavington, Wilts, whose distinguished piety and moral excellence furnished Miss H. Moore with materials for her much admired story of 'The Shepherd of Salisbury Plain.' The dimness of his sight had obliged him to give up his occupation, which he had followed for more than half a century on the same farm, until about six months back:— since which time several respectable farmers, who well knew his worth, entertained him, by rotation, at their houses; and as a mark of their unfeigned respect for his memory, they had his remains conveyed from the place of his decease to his own parish, and buried with more than common, solemnity."

THE LETTER WRITTEN BY DAVID SANDERS, THE SHEPHERD OF SALISBURY PLAIN

Littleton, Aug. 16, 1792.

Dear Friend,

I received a kind and welcome letter from you, dated July 25; which letter I could not answer myself, by reason of the infirmities and weakness of body I was then under; but I desired friend Wastfield, of Imber, to answer it in my stead; and I hope you received it to your satisfaction; but not having since heard from you, I concluded the hurry of harvest prevented. I then acquainted you, my cousin James Saunders was coming at Michaelmas to be your servant, if God shall permit; but he desired a protection from you, that he might come safely from Salisbury to you, and not be molested by the press-gang; for hearing lately of many instances that have happened, he says, he is afraid, not being used to travel; and being a mother's delight, she will not be satisfied: so I hope you will let him know how he may come safely. I hope he will answer to your satisfaction; for he says, he will endeavor to the utmost of his power. You must excuse his spiritual ignorance, for he never had any instruction; and may the Lord open his understanding, and teach him to know his blessed will! I am ready to conclude he will be a good servant; for I am near him, and do not see but he is very diligent, and understands his business. He says, he cannot afford to come under eight guineas a year; and he will put a helping hand to forward his master's business, so far as not to neglect the flock when under his care.—I could wish a few books amongst you, lately wrote by friend Wastfield. I have dispersed many of them; and they are liked much. They are wrote in a simple and innocent style, to promote the glory of God. They are entitled, "The Gospel-Mirror, both to Professor and Profane."

As for my part, I am but very poorly in body, having very sore legs; and cannot perform the business of my flock without help. As to the things of this world, I have but little share, having my little cot to pray and praise my God in, and a bed to rest on: so I have just as much of the world as I desire. But my garment is worn out, and some of my Christian friends think they must put their mites together and buy me one, or else I shall not be able to endure the cold in the winter: so I can say, Good is the Lord! he is still fulfilling his promise: "I will never leave thee, nor forsake thee."

When I read in your last, the tender humility the Lord, by his grace, has wrought in your soul, in bringing you to sit down among the Magdalen and Jerusalem sinners, my aged soul praised God on your behalf; for it is such sinners as Jesus Christ came to seek and save. For he says, "I came not to call the righteous, but sinners to repentance;" therefore, let me, as a wellwisher to your soul, intreat you to yield yourself up to God. Let him have the whole pre-eminence to reign and rule over you, that, as he has begun the work of grace and salvation in your soul, he may carry it on till the day of the Lord Jesus; and you can truly and experimentally say, with the apostle, You have found redemption in his blood, even the forgiveness of sins; "for in the Lord have I found righteousness and strength; and in the Lord doth my heart rejoice, give praise, and give glory; for in his holy name have I found everlasting strength!" Beware, beware of the flattering deluding world, lest you again be shorn of your strength; and, like Samson, become weak as another man, and have no strength nor power to resist the enemy: for here we are in an enemy's country, and have great need to put on the whole armor of God, that we may be able to resist the powerful force of the enemy; for by them we are beset, before and behind, within and without: so I find no way to conquer or overcome, but by fervent prayer in the Spirit, looking unto Jesus, "for he is our great High Priest, exalted and seated at the right hand of God, to be a Prince and a Saviour to all that, by faith, look unto him:" for he hath told us he hath overcome the world; and whosoever, by faith, looketh unto him, shall receive power to overcome all things. I think St. Peter saith, "Unto them that believe, Christ is precious;" and my soul can evidence that he is precious;—more precious than rubies, or the gold wedge of Ophir. Glory be unto his holy name! he is the joy and rejoicing of my heart. For, as the Psalmist saith, "Whom, Lord, have I in Heaven but thee? and there is none on the earth that I desire in comparison of thee!" Oh! that I could leave this corrupted body and fly to my beloved, and enjoy the fulness of divine love. Here, by faith, we behold him through the veil of ordinances; but ere long the veil will be taken away, and ordinances cease. And oh! what joy to think we shall see him face to face; and hear him say unto us, "Ye are they that have continued with me in my temptations, now come and receive a never-fading crown of my glory, and reign with me for ever and ever." The poet says,

> "Earth's but a sorry tent,
>   Pitch'd for a few frail days;
> A short leas'd tenement;
>   Heaven's my song, my praise!
> Oh, happy place! When will it be
> That I shall reign with Christ in thee?"

Now, my dear friend, my heart is enlarged with tender affections of love towards you. Perhaps it may be the last time I shall be ever able to take pen in hand: as you are much my superior, bear with my weakness and simpleness this once, and suffer me to speak the whole of my soul, and deal plainly in asking a few important questions. I am not going to ask you, What denomination or party you hold with? I will leave to yourself to be fully persuaded in your own mind. Is it the desire of your soul to be saved by Jesus Christ, in his own and appointed way, disclaiming or renouncing all help in yourself, relying alone on him for salvation, sinking in the gulph of woe, and, like Peter, crying, "Lord, save, or I perish,"—or the penitent publican, "God be merciful to me a poor sinner,"—feeling yourself (as the prophet Isaiah describeth) "from the crown of the head unto the sole of the foot, to be nothing but wounds, bruises, and putrifying sores;" and so far putrified, that no remedy will do but the blood of the precious Lamb of God, once shed on Calvary, when he there opened a fountain for sin and uncleanness; and that unless, by faith, that balmy blood be applied to your wounded conscience, you must perish everlastingly?—For Jesus Christ is the only

Physician of all wounded sin-sick souls; and what thanks, what praises shall we return unto our God for providing us such a good and able Physician, who is able to save to the uttermost all that, by faith, come unto him! For he healeth all diseases of what kind soever they be; and he for ever liveth to do his needy creatures good. He kindly inviteth us, saying, "Come unto me all ye that labour and are heavy laden, and I will give you rest. Take my yoke upon you, and learn of me, and you shall find rest unto your souls; for my yoke is easy, and my burden light." If all these kind invitations will not encourage us to come and be healed by this kind Physician, I know not what will. He doth not require any pay; for he saith, "If any man will, let him come and take of the water of life freely, without money and without price." He is not in one office only, but in every thing we stand in need of. He is our wisdom to teach us,— to make us wise to everlasting salvation; our righteousness, in our stead, before God; our sanctification before his Heavenly Father, to make us acceptable in his sight, and to answer for us, and make a full satisfaction for the multiplicity of our imperfections; and our redemption, to make us fully complete and acceptable in his sight. Oh wonderful love! Jesus, what hast thou bestowed on such a worm as me! What compassion hast thou shewed to draw me after thee!

> "If still to me thy bowels move,
> Help me to taste thy dying love."

Come on then, dear soul, haste to Jesus; escape for your life; tarry no longer in the horrible city, lest the avenger overtake you and bind you as a prisoner, and deliver you to the judge, and the judge deliver you to the officer, and you be cast into prison, there to lie till you have paid injured justice; which never can, nor ever will be to all eternity. Therefore, delays are dangerous. David said, "I made haste, and delayed not to keep thy righteous commandments." And elsewhere he said, "I will not come into my house, nor suffer my eyes to sleep, nor eye-lids to slumber, till I have found a habitation for the God of Jacob to dwell in."

As the Lord has created an appetite in your soul, let no external or outward forms of religion without the power, satisfy you. Think nothing too much to part with for Christ; for, saith he, "Except a man sell all that he hath, he cannot be my disciple; and whosoever loveth father or mother, wife or child, more than me, is not worthy of me: for whosoever loveth his life shall lose it; and whosoever loseth his life for my sake and the gospel's, shall find it in the life eternal. For what is a man profited, if he should gain the whole world, and lose his own soul? or what shall he give in exchange for his soul?"

I must conclude. May the Lord bless what I have now feebly attempted to speak to you, unto your precious and immortal soul, and make each of us heirs of everlasting life and glory! so, prays your unworthy servant,—Please to give my dutiful respects to Mr. C—; and acquaint him, that I hope he is making sure work of his soul's salvation, for the day is far spent, and the night is at hand; and the wise man adviseth, "whatsoever thy hand findeth to do, do it with all thy might, for there is no knowledge, wisdom, nor device, in the grave, whither thou goest." Beware of the world's flatteries; for, I believe, it has beguiled thousands of poor souls with its flattering delusions; labouring to catch at a shadow, they have lost the substance, still busying themselves with labour and toil after perishing things;—like Martha, much encumbered; while Mary sat at Jesus' feet and heard his words (and so the blessed Jesus declared) that one thing needful: she had chose the good part that never should be taken from her. I do not say we are to be idiots, and care nothing about the world; for the apostle saith, "Be not slothful in business, but fervent in spirit, serving the Lord."—And the Lord saith, "Seek ye first the kingdom of God and his righteousness, and all needful things shall be added unto you." Let him, and each of us, beware we do not lose sight of Jesus, but carefully follow his footsteps; for, saith he, "I am the way, the truth, and the life. If any man follow me; where I am, there shall my servant be also."

My dear friends, I see such beauty in the looks of his love, that I know not how to drop my pen from earnestly desiring you to go unto him, without the camp, bearing his reproach. "Let the dead bury their dead;"—everlasting life is before us:

> "Ere long we shall fly
> To the regions on high,
> For Israel's strength cannot vary nor lie:
> He soon shall appear,
> He more than draws near;
> Our Jesus is come, and eternity's here!"

Farewell; and may the God of peace and love be with you all! so prays, your sincere friend and wellwisher, for my dear Lord and Master Jesus Christ's sake,

DAVID SAUNDERS.

A MEMOIR OF
SIR JAMES STONHOUSE[*]

STONHOUSE (Sir JAMES), a pious and worthy baronet, originally a physician and afterwards a divine, was the son of Richard and Caroline Stonhouse, of Tubney, near Abingdon, in Berkshire, and was born July 20, 1716. His father, who died when his son was ten years old, was, as sir James informs us, "a country squire, kept a pack of hounds, and was a violent Jacobite." Our author succeeded to the title of baronet late in life, by the death of his collateral relation sir James Stonhouse of Radley.

He was educated at Winchester-school, and was afterwards of St. John's college, Oxford, where he took his master's degree in 1739, and his degrees in medicine, M. B. in 1742, and M. D. in 1745. He had his medical education under Dr. Frank Nichols (See F. NICHOLS), whom he represents as a professed deist, and fond of instilling pernicious principles into the minds of his pupils. Mr. Stonhouse resided with him in his house in Lincoln's-inn-fields for two years, and dissected with him, which, he says, was a great and an expensive privilege. He also attended St. Thomas's hospital for two years under those eminent physicians sir Edward Wilmot, Dr. Hall, and Dr. Letherland. Two years more he devoted to medical study and

---

[*] Alexander Chalmers, "The General Biographical Dictionary" (London: J. Nichols, 1812–1816), 435.

observation at Paris, Lyons, Montpellier, and Marseilles. On his return, he settled one year at Coventry, where he married Miss Anne Neale, the eldest of the two daughters of John Neale, esq. of Allesley, near Coventry, and member of parliament for that city. This lady, who died in 1747, soon after their marriage, in the twenty-fifth year of her age, is introduced as one of the examples of frail mortality in Hervey's "Meditations," and is farther commemorated there in a note.

From Coventry, Dr. Stonhouse removed, in 1743, to Northampton, where and through the neighbourhood for many miles, his practice became most extensive; and his benevolence keeping pace with his profits, he was acknowledged in all respects a great benefactor to the poor. Among other schemes for their relief he founded the coun-ty-infirmary at Northampton, but amidst much opposition. During his residence here the celebrated Dr. Akenside endeavoured to obtain a settlement as a practitioner, but found it in vain to interfere with Dr. Stonhouse, who then, as Dr. Johnson observes in his life of Akenside, "practised with such reputation and success, that a stranger was not likely to gain ground upon him."

After practising at Northampton for twenty years, he quitted his profession, assigning for a reason that his practice was become too extensive for his time and health, and that all his attempts to bring it into narrower limits, without giving offence, and occasioning very painful reflec-tions, had failed. But neither the natural activity of his mind, nor his unceasing wish to be doing good, would permit him to remain unemployed, and as his turn of mind was peculiarly bent on subjects of divinity, he determined to go into the church, and was accordingly ordained deacon by the special favour of the bishop of Hereford, in Hereford cathedral, and priest next week by letters dimissory to the bishop of Bristol, in Bristol cathedral, no one, he informs us, being ordained at either of those times but himself. In May 1764 lord Radnor found him very ill at Bristol-wells, and gave him the living of Little-Cheverel; and in December 1779 his lordship's successor gave him that of Great Cheverel.

About ten years before this, he married his second wife Sarah, an heiress, the only child of Thomas Ekins, esq. of Chester-on-the-water, in Northamptonshire. She was left by her father under the guardianship of Dr. Doddridge, who died before she came of age, at which last period Dr. Stonhouse married her. Dr. Stonhouse's piety, for which he was most admired, had not always been uniform. He tells us, that he imbibed erroneous notions from Dr. Nichols, and that he was for seven years a confirmed infidel, and did all he could to subvert Christianity. He went so far as to write a keen pamphlet against it; the *third* edition of which he burnt. He adds, "for writing and spreading of which, I humbly hope, as I have deeply repented of it, God has forgiven me: though I never can forgive myself." His conversion to Christianity, which he attributes to some of Dr. Doddridge's writings, and the various circumstances attending it, were such, that he was advised to write the history of his life, which he accordingly did, and intended it to have been published after his death: but in consequence of the suggestion of a friend, and his own suspicions lest a bad use might have been made of it, he was induced to destroy the manuscript.

After being settled at Cheverel, he applied himself to the duties of his station with fervour and assiduity, and became very popular as a preacher. Much of his general character and conduct, his sentiments and the vicissitudes of his professional employment, may be learned from his correspondence lately published. He died at Bristol-Wells Dec. 8, 1795, in the eightieth year of his age, and was buried in the Wells chapel, in the same grave with his second wife, who died seven years before, over which, on an elegant monument, is an epitaph, in verse, by Miss Hannah More.

Among other ways of doing good, Sir James Stonhouse was convinced that the dispersion of plain and familiar tracts on important subjects, was one of the most important, and accordingly wrote several of these, the greater part of which have been adopted by the Society for Promoting Christian Knowledge. The others are,

1. "Considerations on some particular sins, and on the means of doing good bodily and spiritually."

2. "St. Paul's Exhortation and motive to support the weak or sick poor, a sermon."

3. "A short explanation of the Sacrament of the Lord's Supper, etc."

4. "Hints to a curate for the management of a parish."

5. "A serious address to the parishioners of Great Cheverel," etc.

'TIS ALL FOR THE BEST

BY

HANNAH MORE

'TIS ALL FOR THE BEST*

"IT is all for the best," said Mrs. Simpson, whenever any misfortune befell her. She had got such a habit of vindicating Providence, that, instead of weeping and wailing under the most trying dispensations, her chief care was to convince herself and others, that however great might be her sufferings, and however little they could be accounted for at present, yet that the Judge of all the earth could not but do right. Instead of trying to clear herself from any possible blame that might attach to her under those misfortunes which, to speak after the manner of men, she might seem not to have *deserved*, she was always the first to justify Him who had inflicted it. It was not that she superstitiously converted every visitation into a *punishment;* she entertained more correct ideas of that God who overrules all events. She knew that some calamities were sent to exercise her faith, others to purify her heart; some to chastise her rebellious will, and all to remind her that this "was not her rest;" that this world was not the scene for the full and final display of retributive justice. The honor of God was dearer to her than her own credit, and her chief desire was to turn all events to his glory.

---

* A profligate wit of a neighboring country having attempted to turn this doctrine into ridicule, under the same title here assumed, it occurred to the author than it might not be altogether useless to illustrate the same doctrine on Christian principles. [The work here alluded to is the "Candide," or the Optimist, of Voltaire; the object of which is not only to ridicule the doctrine of providence, but to confound all distinction between good and evil, virtue and vice.]

Though Mrs. Simpson was the daughter of a clergyman, and the widow of a genteel tradesman, she had been reduced, by a succession of misfortunes, to accept of a room in an alms-house. Instead of repining at the change, instead of dwelling on her former gentility, and saying, "How handsomely she had lived once; and how hard it was to be reduced; and she little thought ever to end her days in an alms-house;" which is the common language of those who were never so well off before; she was thankful that such an asylum was provided for want and age; and blessed God that it was to the Christian dispensation alone that such pious institutions owed their birth.

One fine evening, as she was sitting reading her Bible on the little bench shaded with honeysuckles, just before her door, who should come and sit down by her but Mrs. Betty, who had formerly been lady's maid at the nobleman's house in the village of which Mrs. Simpson's father had been minister. Betty, after a life of vanity, was, by a train of misfortunes, brought to this very alms-house; and though she had taken no care, by frugality and prudence, to avoid it, she thought it a hardship and disgrace, instead of being thankful, as she ought to have been, for such a retreat. At first, she did not know Mrs. Simpson; her large bonnet, cloak, and brown stuff gown (for she always made her appearance conform to her circumstances), being very different from the dress she had been used to wear when Mrs. Betty had seen her dining at the great house; and time and sorrow had much altered her countenance. But when Mrs. Simpson kindly addressed her as an old acquaintance, she screamed with surprise—

"What! you, madam?" cried she; "you in an alms-house,

ONE FINE EVENING SHE WAS READING HER BIBLE.

living on charity; you, who used to be so charitable your-self, that you never suffered any distress in the parish, which you could prevent?"

"That may be one reason, Betty," replied Mrs. Simpson, "why Providence has provided this refuge for my old age. And my heart overflows with gratitude, when I look back on his goodness."

"No such great goodness, methinks," said Betty; "why,

you were born and bred a lady, and are now reduced to live in an alms-house."

"Betty, I was born and bred a sinner, undeserving of the mercies I have received."

"No such great mercies," said Betty. "Why, I heard that you had been turned out of doors; that your husband had broke; and that you had been in danger of starving, though I did not know what was become of you."

"It is all true, Betty; glory be to God! it is all true."

"Well," said Betty, "you are an odd sort of a gentlewoman. If, from a prosperous condition, I had been made a bankrupt, a widow, and a beggar, I should have thought it no such mighty matter to be thankful for; but there is no accounting for taste. The neighbors used to say that all your troubles must needs be a judgment upon you; but I, who knew how good you were, thought it very hard you should suffer so much; but now I see you reduced to an alms-house,—I beg your pardon, madam, but I am afraid the neighbors were in the right, and that so many misfortunes could never have happened to you without you had committed a great many sins to deserve them; for I always thought that God is so just, that he *punishes us for all our bad actions, and rewards us for all our good ones*."

"So he does, Betty; but he does it in his own way, and at his own time, and not according to our notions of good and evil; for his ways are not as our ways. God, indeed, punishes the bad, and rewards the good; but he does not do it fully and finally in this world. Indeed, he does not set such a value on outward things as to make riches, and rank, and beauty, and health, the rewards of piety; that would be acting like weak and erring men, and not like a just and holy God. Our belief in a future state of rewards and punishments is not always so strong as it ought to be, even now; but how totally would our faith fail, if we regularly saw every thing made even in this world! We shall lose nothing by having pay-day put off. The longest voyages make the best returns. So far am I from thinking that God is less just, and future happiness less certain, because I see the wicked sometimes prosper, and the righteous suffer in this world, that I am rather led to believe that God is more just, and heaven more certain; for, in the first place, God will not put off his favorite children with so poor a lot as the good things of this world; and next, seeing that the best men here below do not often attain to the best things, why, it only serves to strengthen my belief that they are not the best things in his eye; and he has most assuredly reserved for those that love him such good things as 'eye hath not seen nor ear heard.'* God, by keeping man in Paradise while he was innocent, and turning him into this world as soon as he had sinned, gave a plain proof that he never intended this world, even in its happiest state, as a place of reward. My father gave me good principles and useful knowledge; and while he taught me, by a habit of constant employment, to be, if I may so say, independent on the world, yet he led me to a constant sense of dependence on God."

"I do not see, however," interrupted Mrs. Betty, "that your religion has been of any use to you. It has been so far from preserving you from trouble, that I think you have had more than the usual share."

---

* 1 Corinthians 2:9—But as it is written, Eye hath not seen, nor ear heard, neither have entered into the heart of man, the things which God hath prepared for them that love him.

"No," said Mrs. Simpson; "nor did Christianity ever pretend to exempt its followers from trouble; this is no part of
the promise. Nay, the contrary is rather stipulated; 'in the
world ye shall have tribulation.'* But if it has not taught
me to escape sorrow, I humbly hope it has taught me how
to bear it. If it has not taught me not to feel, it has taught
me not to murmur.—I will tell you a little of my story. As
my father could save little or nothing for me, he was very
desirous of seeing me married to a young gentleman in the
neighborhood, who expressed a regard for me. But while he
was anxiously engaged in bringing this about, my good
father died."

"How very unlucky!" interrupted Betty.

"No, Betty," replied Mrs. Simpson, "it was very providen-
tial; this man, though he maintained a decent character,
had a good fortune, and lived soberly, yet he would not have
made me happy."

"Why, what could you want more of a man?" said Betty.

"Religion," returned Mrs. Simpson. "As my father made a
creditable appearance, and was very charitable, and as I
was an only child, this gentleman concluded that he could
give me a considerable fortune; for he did not know that all
the poor in his parish are the children of every pious
clergyman. Finding I had little or nothing left me, he
withdrew his attentions."

"What a sad thing!" cried Betty.

"No, it was all for the best; Providence overruled his
covetousness to my good. I could not have been happy with
a man whose soul was set on the perishable things of this
world; nor did I esteem him, though I labored to submit my

---

* John 16:33—These things I have spoken unto you, that in me ye might have peace. In
the world ye shall have tribulation: but be of good cheer; I have overcome the world.

own inclinations to those of my kind father. The very circumstance of being left penniless produced the direct contrary effect on Mr. Simpson: he was a sensible young man, engaged in a prosperous business: we had long highly valued each other; but while my father lived, he thought me above his hopes. We were married; I found him an amiable, industrious, good-tempered man; he respected religion and religious people; but, with excellent disposi-tions, I had the grief to find him less pious than I had hoped. He was ambitious, and a little too much immersed in worldly schemes; and though I knew it was all done for my sake, yet that did not blind me so far as to make me think it right. He attached himself so eagerly to business, that he thought every hour lost in which he was not doing something that would tend to raise me to what he called my proper rank. The more prosperous he grew, the less religious he became; and I began to find that one might be unhappy with a husband one tenderly loved. One day, as he was standing on some steps to reach down a parcel of goods, he fell from the top, and broke his leg in two places."

"What a dreadful misfortune!" said Mrs. Betty. "What a signal blessing!" said Mrs. Simpson. "Here I am sure I had reason to say all was for the best; from that very hour in which my outward troubles began, I date the beginning of my happiness. Severe suffering, a near prospect of death, ab-sence from the world, silence, reflection, and, above all, the divine blessing on the prayers and scriptures I read to him, were the means used by our merciful Father to turn my husband's heart. During this confinement, he was awakened to a deep sense of his own sinfulness, of the vanity of all this world has to bestow, and of his great need of a Savior. It was many months before he could leave his bed; during which time his business was neglected; his principal clerk took advantage of his absence, to receive large sums of money in his name, and absconded. On hearing of this great loss, our creditors came faster upon us than we could answer their demands; they grew more impatient, as we were less able to satisfy them; one misfortune followed another, till at length Mr. Simpson became a bankrupt."

"What an evil!" exclaimed Mrs. Betty.

"Yet it led in the end to much good," resumed Mrs. Simpson. "We were forced to leave the town in which we had lived with so much credit and comfort, and to betake ourselves to a mean lodging in a neighboring village, till my husband's strength should be recruited, and till we could have time to look about us, and see what was to be done. The first night we got to this poor dwelling, my husband felt very sorrowful, not for his own sake, but that he had brought so much poverty on me, whom he had so dearly loved: I, on the contrary, was unusually cheerful; for the blessed change in his mind had more than reconciled me to the sad change in his circumstances. I was contented to live with him in a poor cottage for a few years on earth, if it might contribute to our spending a blessed eternity together in heaven. I said to him, 'Instead of lamenting that we are now reduced to want all the comforts of life, I have sometimes been almost ashamed to live in the full enjoyment of them, when I have reflected that my Savior not only chose to deny himself all these enjoyments, but even to live a life of hardship for my sake: not one of his numerous miracles tended to his own comfort; and though we read, at different times, that he both hungered and thirsted, yet it was not for his own gratification that he once changed water into wine; and I have often been struck with the near position of that chapter in which this miracle is recorded, to that in which he thirsted for a draught of water at the well of Samaria.* It was for others, not himself, that even the humble sustenance of barley bread was multiplied. See here, we have a bed left us; I had, indeed, nothing but straw to stuff it with, but the Savior of the world "had not where to lay his head."† My husband smiled through his tears, and we sat down to supper. It consisted of a roll and a bit of cheese which I had brought with me, and we ate it thankfully. Seeing Mr. Simpson beginning to relapse into distrust, the following conversation, as nearly as I can remember, took place between us.

"He began by remarking, that it was a mysterious Providence that he had been less prosperous since he had been less attached to the world, and that his endeavors had not been followed by that success which usually attends industry.—

"I took the liberty to reply: 'Your heavenly Father sees on which side your danger lies, and is mercifully bringing you, by these disappointments, to trust less in the world, and more in himself. My dear Mr. Simpson,' added I, 'we trust every body but God. As children, we obey our parents implicitly, because we are taught to believe all is for our good which they command or forbid. If we undertake a voyage, we trust entirely to the skill and conduct of the pilot; we never torment ourselves with thinking that he

---

* See John 2 and John 4.
† Matthew 8:20—And Jesus saith unto him, The foxes have holes, and the birds of the air have nests; but the Son of man hath not where to lay his head.

will carry us east when he has promised to carry us west. If a dear and tried friend makes us a promise, we depend on him for the performance, and do not wound his feelings by our suspicions. When you used to go your annual journey to London in the mail-coach, you confided yourself to the care of the coachman, that he would carry you where he had engaged to do so; you were not anxiously watching him, and distrusting and inquiring at every turning. When the doctor sends home your medicine, don't you so fully trust in his ability and good will, that you swallow it down in full confidence? You never think of inquiring what are the ingredients, why they are mixed in that particular way, why there is more of one and less of another, and why they are bitter instead of sweet? If one dose does not cure you, he orders another, and changes the medicine when he sees the first does you no good, or that, by long use, the same medicine has lost its effect; if a weaker fails, he prescribes a stronger; you swallow all, you submit to all, never questioning the skill or the kindness of the physician.—God is the only being whom we do not trust, though he is the only one who is fully competent, both in will and power, to fulfill all his promises; and who has solemnly and repeatedly pledged himself to fulfill them, in those Scriptures which we receive as his revealed will.'

"Mr. Simpson thanked me for my little sermon, as he called it; but said, at the same time, that what made my exhortations produce a powerful effect on his mind was, the patient cheerfulness with which he was pleased to say I bore my share in our misfortunes. A submissive behavior, he said, was the best practical illustration of a real faith.

"When we had thanked God for our supper, we prayed

together; after which we read the eleventh chapter of the
Epistle to the Hebrews. When my husband had finished it,
he said, 'Surely, if God's chief favorites have been martyrs,
is not that a sufficient proof that this world is not a place
of happiness, nor earthly prosperity the reward of virtue?
Shall we, after reading this chapter, complain of our petty
trials? Shall we not rather be thankful that our affliction is
so light?'

"Next day, Mr. Simpson walked out in search of some
employment, by which he might be supported. He got a
recommendation to Mr. Thomas, an opulent farmer and
factor, who had large concerns, and wanted a skilful person to assist him in keeping his accounts. This we thought
a fortunate circumstance; for we found that the salary
would serve to procure us at least all the necessaries of
life. The farmer was so pleased with Mr. Simpson's quick-
ness, regularity, and good sense, that he offered us, of his
own accord, a little neat cottage of his own, which then
happened to be vacant, and told us we should live rent-
free, and promised to be a friend to us."

"All *does* seem for the best now, indeed," interrupted
Mrs. Betty.

"We shall see," said Mrs. Simpson, and thus went on:—

"I now became very easy and very happy, and was
cheerfully employed in putting our few things in order,
and making every thing look to the best advantage. My
husband, who wrote all the day for his employer, in the
evenings assisted me in doing up our little garden. This
was a source of much pleasure to us; we both loved a
garden, and we were not only contented, but cheerful. Our
employer had been absent some weeks on his annual

"WE BOTH LOVED A GARDEN."

journey. He came home on a Saturday night, and the next morning sent for Mr. Simpson to come and settle his accounts, which were got behindhand by his long absence. We were just going to church, and Mr. Simpson sent back word, that he would call and speak to him on his way home. A second message followed, ordering him to come to the farmer's directly. We agreed that we would walk round that way, and that my husband should call, and excuse his attendance.

"The farmer, more ignorant and worse educated than his ploughmen, with all that pride and haughtiness which the possession of wealth, without knowledge or religion, is apt to give, rudely asked my husband what he meant, by sending him word that he could not come to him till the next day, and insisted that he should stay and settle the accounts then.

"'Sir,' said my husband, in a very respectful manner, 'I am on my road to church, and am afraid I shall be too late.'

"'Are you so?' said the farmer. 'Do you know who sent for you? You may, however, go to church, if you will, so you make haste back; and, d'ye hear, you may leave your accounts with me, as I conclude you have brought them with you; I will look them over by the time you return, and then you and I can do all I want to have done today, in about a couple of hours; and I will give you home some letters to copy for me in the evening.'

"'Sir,' answered my husband, 'I dare not obey you; it is Sunday.'

"'And so you refuse to settle my accounts only because it is Sunday?'

"'Sir,' replied Mr. Simpson, 'if you would give me a handful of silver and gold, I dare not break the commandment of my God.'

"'Well,' said the farmer, 'but this is not breaking the commandment; I don't order you to drive my cattle, or to work in my garden, or to do any thing which you might fancy would be a bad example.'

"'Sir,' replied my husband, 'the example indeed goes a great way, but it is not the first object. The deed is wrong in itself.'

"'Well, but I shall not keep you from church; and when you have been there, there is no harm in doing a little business, or taking a little pleasure, the rest of the day.'

"'Sir,' answered my husband, 'the commandment does not say, Thou shalt keep holy the Sabbath *morning*, but the Sabbath *day*.'

"'Get out of my house, you puritanical rascal, and out of

my cottage too,' said the farmer; 'for if you refuse to do my work, I am not bound to keep my engagement with you; as you will not obey me as a master, I shall not pay you as a servant.'

"'Sir,' said Mr. Simpson, 'I would gladly obey you, but I have a Master in heaven, whom I dare not disobey.'

"'Then let him find employment for you,' said the enraged farmer; 'for I fancy you will get but poor employment on earth with these scrupulous notions; and so send home my papers directly, and pack off out of the parish.'

"'Out of your cottage,' said my husband, 'I certainly will; but as to the parish, I hope I may remain in that, if I can find employment.'

"'I will make it too hot to hold you,' replied the farmer; 'so you had better troop off, bag and baggage; for I am overseer, and as you are sickly, it is my duty not to let any vagabonds stay in the parish who are likely to become chargeable.'

"By the time my husband returned home,—for he found it too late to go to church,—I had got our little dinner ready; it was a better one than we had for a long while been accustomed to see, and I was unusually cheerful at this improvement in our circumstances. I saw his eyes full of tears; and O! with what pain did he bring himself to tell me that it was the last dinner we must ever eat in that house! I took his hand with a smile, and only said, 'The Lord gave, and the Lord taketh away; blessed be the name of the Lord.'—

"'Notwithstanding this sudden stroke of injustice,' said my husband, 'this is still a happy country. Our employer, it is true, may turn us out at a moment's notice, because the cottage is his own, but he has no further power over us; he cannot confine or punish us. His riches, it is true, give him power to insult, but not to oppress us. The same laws to which the affluent resort, protect *us* also. And as to our being driven out from a cottage, how many persons of the highest rank have lately been driven out from their palaces and castles!* Persons, too, born in a station which we never enjoyed, and used to all the indulgences of that rank and wealth we never knew, are at this moment wandering over the face of the earth, without a house and without bread; exiles and beggars; while we, blessed be God, are in our own native land; we have still our liberty, our limbs, the protection of just and equal laws, our churches, our Bibles, and our Sabbaths.'

"This happy state of my husband's mind hushed my sorrows, and I never once murmured; nay, I sat down to dinner with a degree of cheerfulness, endeavoring to cast all our care on 'Him that careth for us.'† We had begged to stay till the next morning, as Sunday was not the day on which we liked to remove; but we were ordered not to sleep another night in that house; so, as we had little to carry, we marched off in the evening to the poor lodging we had before occupied. The thought that my husband had cheerfully renounced his little all for conscience' sake, gave an unspeakable serenity to my mind; and I felt thankful, that, though cast down, we were not forsaken; nay, I felt a lively gratitude to God, that, while I doubted not he would accept this little sacrifice, as it was heartily made for his sake, he had graciously forborne to call us to greater trials."

---

* By the French revolution. This most edifying tale was printed when the nobles and clergy of that country were either in dungeons waiting for the scaffold, or in banishment subsisting on the charity of strangers.

† 1 Peter 5:7—Casting all your care upon him; for he careth for you.

"And so you were turned adrift once more? Well, ma'am, saving your presence, I hope you won't be such a fool as to say *all was for the best* NOW."

"Yes, Betty, He who does all things well, now made his kind providence more manifest than ever. That very night, while we were sweetly sleeping in our poor lodging, the pretty cottage out of which we were so unkindly driven, was burnt to the ground by a flash of lightning, which caught the thatch, and so completely consumed the whole little building, that, had it not been for that merciful Providence who thus overruled the cruelty of the farmer for the preservation of our lives, we must have been burned to ashes with the house. 'It was the Lord's doing, and it was marvelous in our eyes.' 'O that men would therefore praise the Lord for his goodness, and for all, the wonders that he doeth for the children of men!'

"I will not tell you all the trials and afflictions which befell us afterwards. I would also spare my heart the sad story of my husband's death."

"Well, that was another blessing too, I suppose," said Betty.

"O, it was the severest trial ever sent me!" replied Mrs. Simpson, a few tears quietly stealing down her face. "I almost sunk under it. Nothing but the abundant grace of God could have carried me through such a visitation: and yet I now feel it to be the greatest mercy I ever experienced; he was my idol; no trouble ever came near my heart while he was with me. I got more credit than I deserved for my patience under trials, which were easily borne, while he who shared and lightened them was spared to me. I had indeed prayed and struggled to be weaned from this world, but still my affection for him tied me down to earth with a strong cord; and though I did earnestly try to keep my eyes fixed on the eternal world, yet I viewed it with too feeble a faith; I viewed it at too great a distance. I found it difficult to realize it. I had deceived myself. I had fancied that I bore my troubles so well from the pure love of God; but I have since found that my love for my husband had too great a share in reconciling me to every difficulty which I underwent for him. I lost him; the charm was broken; the cord which tied me down to earth was cut; this world had nothing left to engage me; Heaven had now no rival in my heart. Though my love of God had always been sincere, yet I found there wanted this blow to make it perfect. But though all that had made life pleasant to me was gone, I did not sink as those who have no hope. I prayed that I might still, in this trying conflict, be enabled to adorn the doctrine of God my Savior.

"After many more hardships, I was at length so happy as to get an asylum in this alms-house. Here my cares are at an end, but not my duties."

"Now you are wrong again," interrupted Mrs. Betty; "your duty is now to take care of yourself; for I am sure you have nothing to spare."

"There you are mistaken again," said Mrs. Simpson. "People are so apt to fancy that money is all in all, that all the other gifts of Providence are overlooked as things of no value. I have here a great deal of leisure; a good part of this I devote to the wants of those who are more distressed than myself. I work a little for the old, and I instruct the young. My eyes are good; this enables me to read the Bible either to those whose sight is decayed, or who were never taught to read. I have tolerable health; so that I am able occasionally to sit up with the sick; in the intervals of nursing, I can pray with them. In my younger days, I thought it not much to sit up late for my pleasure; shall I now think much of sitting up now and then to watch by a dying bed? My Savior waked and watched for me in the garden and on the mount; and shall I do nothing for his suffering members? It is only by keeping his sufferings in view, that we can truly practice charity to others, or exercise self-denial to ourselves."

"Well," said Mrs. Betty, "I think if I had lived in such genteel life as you have done, I could never be reconciled to an alms-house; and I am afraid I should never forgive any of those who were the cause of sending me there, particularly that farmer Thomas, who turned you out of doors."

"Betty," said Mrs. Simpson, "I not only forgive him heartily, but I remember him in my prayers, as one of those instruments with which it has pleased God to work for my good. O! never put off forgiveness to a dying bed! When people come to die, we often see how the conscience is troubled with sins of which before they hardly felt the existence. How ready are they to make restitution of ill-gotten gain! and this, perhaps, for two reasons; from a feeling conviction that it can be of no use to them where they are going, as well as from a near view of their own responsibility. We also hear, from the most hardened, of death-bed forgiveness of enemies. Even malefactors at Tyburn* forgive. But why must we wait for a dying bed, to do what ought to be done now? Believe me, that scene will be so full of terror and amazement to the soul, that we had not need load it with unnecessary business."

---

* Tyburn—a place of public executions.

Just as Mrs. Simpson was saying these words, a letter was brought her from the minister of the parish where the farmer lived, by whom Mr. Simpson had been turned out of his cottage. The letter was as follows:—

"MADAM,

"I write to tell you that your old oppressor, Mr. Thomas, is dead. I attended him in his last moments. O, may my latter end never be like his! I shall not soon forget his despair at the approach of death. His riches, which had been his sole joy, now doubled his sorrows; for he was going where they could be of no use to him; and he found, too late, that he had laid up no treasure in heaven. He felt great concern at his past life, but for nothing more than his unkindness to Mr. Simpson. He charged me to find you out, and let you know, that by his will he bequeathed you five hundred pounds, as some compensation. He died in great agonies; declaring, with his last breath, that if he could live his life over again, he would serve God, and strictly observe the Sabbath.

"Yours, etc.

"J. JOHNSON."

Mrs. Betty, who had listened attentively to the letter, jumped up, clapped her hands, and cried out, "Now all *is for the best*, and I shall see you a lady once more."

"I am, indeed, thankful for this mercy," said Mrs. Simpson, "and am glad that riches were not sent me till I had learned, as I humbly hope, to make a right use of them. But come, let us go in, for I am very cold, and find I have sat too long in the night air."

Betty was now ready enough to acknowledge the hand of Providence in this prosperous event, though she was blind

"NOW ALL IS FOR THE BEST."

to it when the dispensation was more dark. Next morning, she went early to visit Mrs. Simpson, but not seeing her below, she went up stairs, where, to her great sorrow, she found her confined to her bed by a fever, caught the night before by sitting so late on the bench, reading the letter, and talking it over.

Betty was now more ready to cry out against Providence than ever. "What! to catch a fever while you were reading that very letter which told you about your good fortune; which would have enabled you to live like a lady, as you are. I never will believe this is for the best—to be deprived of life, just as you were beginning to enjoy it!"

"Betty," said Mrs. Simpson, "we must learn not to rate health nor life itself too highly. There is little in life, for its own sake, to be so fond of. As a good archbishop used to say, 'tis but the same thing over again, or probably worse; so

many more nights and days, summers and winters; a repe-
tition of the same pleasures, but with less relish for them; a
return of the same or greater pains, but with less strength,
and perhaps less patience, to bear them."

"Well," replied Betty, "I did think that Providence was
at last giving you your reward."

"Reward!" cried Mrs. Simpson. "O, no! my merciful Father will not put me off with so poor a portion as wealth; I
feel I shall die."

"It is very hard, indeed," said Betty, "so good as you are,
to be taken off just as your prosperity was beginning."

"You think I am good just now," said Mrs. Simpson, "because I am prosperous. Success is no sure mark of God's
favor; at this rate, you, who judge by outward things,
would have thought Herod a better man than John the
Baptist; and if I may be allowed to say so, you, on your
principles, that the sufferer is the sinner, would have
believed Pontius Pilate higher in God's favor than the
Savior whom he condemned to die for your sins and mine."

In a few days, Mrs. Betty found that her new friend was
dying, and though she was struck at her resignation, she
could not forbear murmuring that so good a woman should
be taken away at the very instant in which she came into
possession of so much money.

"Betty," said Mrs. Simpson in a feeble voice, "I believe
you love me dearly; you would do any thing to cure me; yet
you do not love me so well as God loves me, though *you*
would raise me up, and He is putting a period to my life.
He has never sent me a single stroke which was not absolutely necessary for me. You, if you could restore me, might
be laying me open to some temptation from which God, by

removing, will deliver me. Your kindness in making this world so smooth for me, I might forever have deplored in a world of misery. God's grace in afflicting me, will hereafter be the subject of my praises in a world of blessedness. Betty," added the dying woman, "do you really think that I am going to a place of rest and joy eternal?"

"To be sure I do," said Betty.

"Do you firmly believe that I am going to the assembly of the first-born; to the spirits of just men made perfect; to God, the Judge of all; and to Jesus, the Mediator of the new covenant?"

"I am sure you are," said Betty.

"And yet," resumed she, "you would detain me from all this happiness; and you think my merciful Father is using me unkindly by removing me from a world of sin, and sorrow, and temptation, to such joys as have not entered into the heart of man to conceive; while it would have better suited your notions of reward to defer my entrance into the blessedness of heaven, that I might have enjoyed a legacy of a few hundred pounds! Believe my dying words— ALL IS FOR THE BEST."

Mrs. Simpson expired soon after, in a frame of mind which convinced her new friend that "God's ways are not as our ways."

www.ingramcontent.com/pod-product-compliance
Lightning Source LLC
Chambersburg PA
CBHW030542130626
46552CB00006B/2378